"Jacinda sees you as my last hope,"

Catherine told Joshua. "She's afraid I'll let you slip through my fingers."

"Why didn't you tell her you have this thing about bankers before she got her hopes up? Didn't you tell her we all foreclose on innocent women and children and take away their homes?"

"I never said that. I know you're just doing your job. I just wish..."

"You wish it weren't my job. Sometimes I wish it weren't, either. If I were a farmer, you would have kissed me today, wouldn't you?"

Catherine's eyes widened and her heart beat out a warning. "Wait a minute. Don't jump to conclusions. I'm not looking for a farmer. I'm not looking for anybody. I admit there may be something between us. I don't understand it, but I don't deny it."

Josh nodded. "Like lightning bolts. You don't have to understand them to feel them when they hit you."

Dear Reader,

August is vacation month, and no matter where you're planning to go, don't forget to take along this month's Silhouette Romance novels. They're the perfect summertime read! And even if you can't get away, you can still escape from it all for a few hours of love and adventure with Silhouette Romance books.

August continues our WRITTEN IN THE STARS series. Each month in 1992 we're proud to present a book that focuses on the hero and his astrological sign. This month we're featuring the proud, passionate Leo man in Suzanne Carey's intensely emotional *Baby Swap*.

You won't want to miss the rest of our fabulous August lineup. We have love stories by Elizabeth August, Brittany Young, Carol Grace and Carla Cassidy. As a special treat, we're introducing a talented newcomer, Sandra Paul. And in months to come, watch for Silhouette Romance novels by many more of your favorite authors, including Diana Palmer, Annette Broadrick and Marie Ferrarella.

The Silhouette Romance authors and editors love to hear from readers and we'd love to hear from *you*.

Happy reading from all of us at Silhouette!

Valerie Susan Hayward
Senior Editor

CAROL GRACE

Home Is Where the Heart Is

Silhouette *Romance*

Published by Silhouette Books New York

America's Publisher of Contemporary Romance

A Note From The Author:

There is no Aruaca, but there is a real Tranquility located in the Central Valley of California, where farmers still earn a living growing cotton, rice and wheat.

For my sister Phyllis who leads a life of adventure and romance any heroine would envy.

SILHOUETTE BOOKS
300 E. 42nd St., New York, N.Y. 10017

HOME IS WHERE THE HEART IS

Copyright © 1992 by Carol Culver

ISBN: 0-373-08882-5

First Silhouette Books printing August 1992

All the characters in this book have no existence outside the imagination of the author and have no relation whatsoever to anyone bearing the same name or names. They are not even distantly inspired by any individual known or unknown to the author, and all incidents are pure invention.

®: Trademark used under license and registered in the United States Patent and Trademark Office and in other countries.

Printed in the U.S.A.

Books by Carol Grace

Silhouette Romance

Make Room for Nanny #690
A Taste of Heaven #751
Home Is Where the Heart Is #882

CAROL GRACE

has always been interested in travel and living abroad. She spent her junior year in college in France and toured the world working on the hospital ship *Hope*. She and her husband spent the first year and a half of their marriage in Iran where they both taught English. Then, with their toddler daughter, they lived in Algeria for two years.

Carol says that writing is another way of making her life exciting. Her office is an Airstream trailer parked behind her mountaintop home, which overlooks the Pacific Ocean and which she shares with her inventor husband, their daughter, who is now sixteen years old, and their eleven-year-old son.

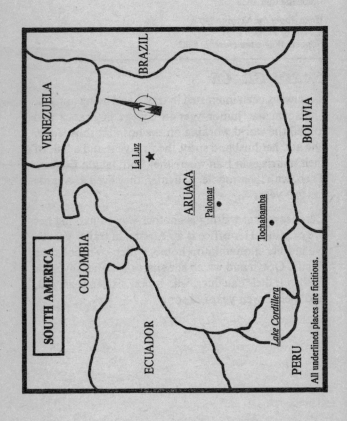

SOUTH AMERICA

VENEZUELA

BRAZIL

COLOMBIA

La Luz ★

ARUACA

Palomar •

ECUADOR

Tochabamba •

Lake Cordillera

PERU

BOLIVIA

All underlined places are fictitious.

Prologue

The sun was merciless in the Central Valley of California in July. Even Catherine Logan, who had spent every summer of her twenty-six years there, felt the dry heat sear through her cotton shirt and shorts. She walked quickly to a seat in the shade under a temporary awning the auctioneers had set up. There were familiar faces in the crowd, but she avoided them as they'd avoided her out of embarrassment or pity for the past six months. It didn't matter.

She would never be able to look them in the eye again. Her parents had sold out. The drought drove people to desperate measures. There were divorces; there had even been a suicide in the next county. Her parents had only sold out. And they weren't the only ones.

For the past three years Catherine had watched the fields she worked being baked dry and saw the worry lines etched in her father's face as he borrowed more and sunk deeper into debt. When the foreclosure notice came, she went to the bank herself, pleading with them to extend the loan, to give them a chance, one year, one growing season to turn the farm around. But the answer had been no.

She swiveled around on the plastic seat of her folding chair. There he was leaning against the barn, conspicuous in a pin-striped suit. The man who had turned her down, old Cyrus Grant, loosened his tie and met her eyes with discomfort.

She turned around abruptly, unable to conceal her anger with him and his bank. It was his decision that had forced her off the land that had been in her family for three generations.

A few minutes later the pharmacist's son and successor, Donny, slid into the seat next to hers. She felt his eyes on her, but she was determined not to let it bother her. If there was anything worse than being ignored, it was being pitied.

"Catherine," he said, mopping his round face with a handkerchief, "why did you come? It's just going to hurt more to see the old place broken up and sold off."

She glanced briefly at his red face, the blue eyes round and curious. "The hurt's gone, Don," she assured him coolly. Replaced by resentment and shame, she thought, the shame of failure. The local girl who had "gone on" and earned a degree couldn't save her parents' farm.

"I had to come today," she continued, "to see it for the last time. My roots are here. *Were* here." She looked out across the dry fields, where stalks of wheat withered in the shimmering heat.

"I just thought it would be easier not to face everybody again...."

"I'm not interested in the easy way," she said, her dark eyes blazing. "If I were, I wouldn't have gone into farming."

He nodded and glanced away. Catherine noticed it was that way with everyone these days. Either they stared or they looked away.

"Looks like a good crowd, though. With what the land brought..." He paused uneasily. "Your folks'll be able to retire."

Catherine didn't tell him that they'd already retired, had bought a duplex in Sacramento six miles from her sister and her children. He must realize that as tired and discouraged as her parents were, they didn't want to retire. Or did they? Had it been relief or regret on their faces the day they had signed the papers?

The auctioneer stepped up to a makeshift podium, adjusted the microphone and began his familiar spiel. The land had already been sold to a developer. Catherine didn't dare look in the direction of the white frame house.

"The livestock brought a fair price," Donny noted, "over in Fresno the other day."

Catherine nodded. The last thing she needed was to think about the calves she had helped bring into the world, the pigs she had named and fed being sold off at the county fairgrounds. It was bad enough to hear the auctioneer describe the combine and the bailer and to hear voices behind her offer half what they were worth. Were the bankers disappointed? Probably not. For them it was just another foreclosure, just another auction, just another family driven off the farm.

She'd never forget Mr. Grant's flat voice, dry as the land itself, as he'd explained why he couldn't lend them any more money. She could still taste the humiliation as he'd explained it to her as if she were a child instead of an adult with a degree from the best university in the state.

She wiped the perspiration from her forehead as the auctioneer directed the buyers' attention to the giant tractor standing in the field behind him, just where her father had left it after he plowed the field for the last time.

"What do I hear for Old Yellow?" the man called out, and Catherine's heart sank. How many times had she sat next to her father on Old Yellow until she was old enough to drive the tractor herself? The metal treads were shiny from years of wear. Even from where she sat she could see the rust spots on the sides. Maybe no one would buy it.

"Don't make 'em like that anymore," Donny said under his breath, and Catherine had to agree. The tractor was one of a kind, and she loved that machine. How she longed to climb up and take the wheel again and smell the rich, damp earth and watch the plow behind her scatter the clumps of dirt.

Someone did buy it, of course, but she didn't turn around to see who it was. Her eyes were fastened on the next item—the flatbed truck. Next to her Donny smiled.

"Now that brings back memories, doesn't it? I remember seeing you hauling fertilizer from the feed and fuel in town. Everybody said your daddy was crazy to let you drive it."

"My father wasn't crazy," she explained softly. "He wanted me to know how to run a farm. Driving a truck or a tractor was part of the education." The rest she'd gotten at the university, the part about hybrids and grain futures. She'd been ready. As prepared as anyone could be to run a farm. But she couldn't fight the drought and the disease, and she couldn't sit here any longer and watch the disintegration of her past and future.

She swallowed hard and stood up, turned and walked past friends and strangers without seeing them, her chin held high and her eyes dry. Let them stare, let them whisper. She could imagine what they were saying. "Poor Catherine . . . nothing left . . . where will she go? What will she do?"

She walked faster as the auctioneer's voice rose to a crescendo. "Going, going, gone," he called as she rounded the empty barn. He could have been talking to her as well as the flatbed. They were both going, but where? She only knew she had to get as far away from Tranquility as she could.

Catherine leaned against the front fence and gave in to the pent-up emotions she had suppressed all morning. Her eyes blinded with tears, she heard the voice echo through the air once more. "Going, going, gone."

Chapter One

The diesel truck bounced up and down on the rocky dirt road, and Catherine Logan gripped the edge of the passenger seat to keep from hitting her head on the roof. Behind her in the long flatbed, where she usually sat, a dozen Mamara Indian women were wedged between burlap sacks bulging with lettuce, parsley and mangoes. She was proud of the harvest, proud of what they'd accomplished with no machinery, and proud of the Aruacan women who worked so hard for so little. So little that at the end of a grueling market day they ended up with no more than a few pesos to show for it. The money the women earned went right through their hands and into the pockets of the workers they depended on to bring the crops to market. Catherine smoothed her layered skirts and turned to face the driver.

"Tomás," she shouted over the roar of the diesel engine, "can't you lower your price for us? These are poor women who can't afford your fees."

Hunched over the wheel, he spoke without looking at her. "And what about me?" he asked. "Do I not have to make a living, too? Do you know the price of a truck these days?"

Catherine shook her head. She had no idea of the price of a truck in Aruaca. She had been a Peace Corps volunteer for eighteen months and she knew the prices of potatoes and bread and shoes, but not trucks. She tapped the driver on the shoulder. "How much," she asked, "for a truck like this?"

"Too much," he replied with a glance over his shoulder, "for them. But for a rich American like you..." He shrugged. "Maybe not."

She grimaced. Despite the fact that she lived in a small house as the other farmers did, dressed like the women in a fringed shawl and wore her hair in a long braid, there were still some local people who thought she must be rich. They didn't know that except for the living allowance the Peace Corps gave her she would be penniless.

As they bumped along the road, Catherine was convinced the village would never rise out of its cycle of unending poverty unless the villagers owned their own truck. But how? Borrowing the money was out of the question. Or was it? The truck swayed as they rounded a narrow curve, and Catherine braced her feet against the floorboard and looked out the window into the steep ravine below. She had never driven on mountain roads like these, but if they had their own truck, she would do it. She would do anything to help these people.

Her eyelids drooped and she stifled a yawn. The women had been up since 3:00 a.m. and only now were they approaching the outskirts of La Luz. By the time the truck rumbled up the hilly streets of the capital, it was six o'clock and the Rodriguez Market was teeming with activity. As soon as Tomás parked the truck, the women trudged from the street to the market, doubled over by the weight of the produce on their backs. Catherine, with her colorful *ahuayo* filled with lettuce, wove her way through the crowds to their stall, a structure of vertical two-by-fours that supported a patched roof of corrugated tin and plastic.

Doña Jacinda, her small face browned and wrinkled from the years in the fields, surveyed the young woman from California and sighed. *"Ah, la Catalina."* She shook her head in mock despair. "What is to become of you buried here among the burlap sacks with only farmers for company? When I was your age, I was married and the mother of six already."

Catherine straightened her bowler hat and smiled. "But, Jacinda, it was you who taught me that 'Women's faults are many, but men have only two. Everything they say and everything they do.'"

A shopper arrived and silenced the unspoken retort in Jacinda's throat. While Catherine watched her haggle over the price of parsley, she surveyed the early-morning bargain hunters. She seldom saw tourists at the market, but over the babble of Spanish came the sound of English, of Americans speaking English. She leaned over the wooden crates to see a small group of men approaching, wearing suits and ties. She hadn't heard a word of English for weeks, not since the last Peace Corps meeting in La Luz. The man in the middle of the group seemed to be the center of attention.

He would be the center of attention anywhere, she decided, with his dark, close-cropped hair and rangy good looks. He moved easily through the throngs of morning shoppers, his suit coat slung over his shoulder. His blue eyes swept the stalls as if he were looking for something special. Guava? Papaya? Handwoven baskets? As he drew closer, he caught Catherine's eye, and she looked away quickly, embarrassed to be caught staring.

Jacinda nudged Catherine with her elbow. A woman wrapped in a tattered shawl with a baby on her back was asking the price of mangoes. Catherine had been so busy watching the man that she hadn't noticed her.

"Do not go lower than three pesos a piece," Jacinda whispered urgently.

Catherine flushed and bit her lip. "Three pesos," she said softly. She could plant, she could plow and she could pick, but she couldn't bargain. For months she had tried to learn, but she always came down too low too fast, or stayed too high too long until her customers shook their heads and went elsewhere. Maybe today, with Jacinda at her side, she could finally get it right.

The customer complained loudly that she couldn't afford to pay that much for a mango, and then her baby started crying.

Out of the corner of her eye Catherine saw the man with the blue eyes at the edge of the crowd regarding her intently. She wiped her damp palms against her skirt and cleared her throat, but no sound came out.

Jacinda, weighing fruit with one hand and making change with the other, was at Catherine's elbow. In a flash she closed the deal, grabbed the mangoes and wrapped them up. The customer paid and walked away grumbling, but Jacinda's black eyes gleamed.

"Did you see that, *chica?*" she asked Catherine. "There was nothing to it. It was a fair price and she knew it. Start high so you have room to come down."

Tiny worry lines etched themselves in Catherine's forehead. The man was now leaning against the stall across from them and still watching her. She looked down at Jacinda. "But she looked so poor, and she has a baby to feed."

Jacinda snorted. "That is not her baby. And she wears those old clothes on market day. I see her every week. Harden your soft heart, Catalina. We will make a bargainer out of you yet."

Catherine nodded. "I just need a little practice." When she glanced up, the man was standing in front of her holding a half-dozen mangoes in his hands, so close she caught the masculine scent of pine soap.

"How much?" he asked in careful Spanish, and Catherine slanted a desperate look in Jacinda's direction. She wasn't ready for another customer yet. And she definitely wasn't ready for the man in front of her whose broad forehead and wide, generous mouth made her heart skip a beat.

Jacinda took in the situation with a flash of her dark eyes and opened her palm as if she were handing the man over to her. This one is for you, she seemed to say. Don't blow it this time.

Catherine took a deep breath and looked up into dazzling blue eyes. "Six pesos each," she said firmly. The sights and the sounds of the market faded except for the beating of Catherine's heart. Start at six and come down to three, she repeated to herself. But the man didn't say anything. How could she come down to three if he didn't speak? He just stood there, holding the mangoes and staring at her until she felt her knees weaken, and she swayed back against a wooden crate.

The man's eyes widened in alarm, and he dropped the mangoes in an effort to steady her. His friends picked up the fruit and advised him to offer two instead of six.

Just as loudly and just as firmly every one of the vendors in Catherine's stall began shouting reasons why the mangoes were worth more. They may not have understood the Americans, but they knew how to keep the bargaining alive. There was a glimmer deep in the man's eyes, and the corner of his mouth twitched. Catherine thought that if he laughed she wouldn't be able to control herself, and then her career as a vendor would be over. Bargaining was serious business, and she knew she was being tested. Right here and right now.

"Six pesos each," she repeated over the hubbub.

Suddenly the stall fell silent. He reached into his pocket for a handful of silver and counted the coins one by one as he placed them in her outstretched palms. His fingers were cool, and she felt the current flow from his hand into hers. Then he carefully closed her hand around the money and held it tightly for a long moment.

There was no amusement in his eyes this time. There was something else, something that caught and held her for longer than the transaction required. His companions were incredulous.

"What is it with you, Bentley? The first woman you see and you lose it."

"Come on, boss. We've got to get you the hell out of here and back to the bank before this woman talks you into a crate of potatoes and we have to store them in the vault."

The women surrounded Catherine to congratulate her. The noise level rose, and when she looked again he was gone. He and his friends had been swallowed up by the crowd. But she had held firm and made a big profit. She had passed the test. She was one of them.

To celebrate, Jacinda took her to the tiny bar-styled café late in the afternoon when the shadows fell over the stall and the other women were packing their empty bags and counting the money. The café was warmly lighted and inviting with the aroma of strong coffee. Jacinda patted a bar stool and motioned for Catherine to sit next to her.

"It was a good day," Jacinda remarked as the proprietor set small cups of black coffee in front of them. "Do you know I have worked in the stalls since I was fourteen years old and I have never seen anyone pay full price for anything? It was most amazing."

"Amazing," Catherine agreed, wrapping her hands around the cup to feel the warmth. "But I can't take full credit, *amiga mia*. The man was North American. Unaccustomed to bargaining. Like me. I'm afraid I won't be able to take advantage of anyone again."

Jacinda picked up her cup and stared thoughtfully at Catherine. "Unless he comes back."

Catherine shook her head. "He's not coming back. Why should he?"

Don Panchito leaned across the counter. "The *norteamericanos* were here also this morning."

Catherine leaned forward on her tall stool. "Is it true they're bankers?"

The old man nodded and refilled Catherine's cup. "The big bank in the middle of town."

Catherine set her cup down on the counter. She swore she would never set foot in another bank again, never speak to another banker. But a loan for a truck would make all the difference to the village. If fate had sent her a banker, could she refuse to go and see Mr. Bentley in his big bank in the middle of town?

Joshua Bentley stood at the window of his office on the twelfth floor of the International Bank Building. Before him lay the city of La Luz spread out like a tapestry woven of poverty and riches. He had only been in the city for two weeks, but it called to him, tempting him to come down out of his lofty tower and rub elbows with the people—people like the woman with the dark eyes and pink cheeks. His eyes sought out the corrugated roofs of the Rodriguez Market, barely visible in the haze. Was she sitting there today with her bowler hat tilted to one side, taking advantage of newcomers again? She hadn't been there yesterday or the day before.

He hadn't minded being taken or laughed at. Maybe it was the altitude that made him feel this way. At twelve thousand feet hallucinations and faulty judgment were common. But women who ignited sparks with a glance weren't common, not in Josh's experience. The phones on his desk rang, the fax machines poured out messages with the prices of gold and silver and yet he stood at the window, wondering where she was and what she was doing.

Finally he could ignore the insistent ring of the telephone no longer. It was the receptionist in the lobby.

"There's an American woman who wants to see you."

"What about?" He shifted impatiently. He had work to do. Never mind that he wasn't doing it.

"She says it's about a loan."

"Send her to the loan department."

"I tried, but she asked for you specifically."

He sighed. Probably the wife of a businessman who had overdrawn her checking account. "Okay, send her up."

In a few minutes his secretary, in her high heels and tailored suit, knocked on his door and gave him a puzzled look. "A woman is here to see you..." she began.

He nodded. "I know." The words died in his throat as she walked into his office. The same woman he'd been thinking about nonstop for the past five days. How in hell had she passed herself off as an American? She was still wearing her ridiculous bowler hat above dark eyes that stared boldly into his.

He was trying to construct a sentence in Spanish, any sentence just to break the silence, but the words wouldn't come and all he could do was point to the chair that faced his desk.

She nodded slightly and carefully folded her long skirt underneath her. Then she pressed her palms together. "I've come to ask for a loan," she said, her unwavering gaze locked with his.

He leaned back against his desk so that he wouldn't fall over. It was the shock of hearing her speak perfect English. If only she hadn't asked for something he couldn't give her.

"Have I come to the right place?" she asked when he didn't say anything.

"Not really," he answered reluctantly. "But no matter where you go the answer is no."

Startled, she stood up. "No? But you haven't even asked me how much I want or what I want it for."

"All right," he agreed. "Tell me how much you want and what you want it for. But first tell me how you happen to speak such good English."

She tossed her long braid over her shoulder, and he thought he saw a glint of amusement in her dark eyes. But when he smiled back it was gone and he was disappointed.

"I'm an American," she said. "In the Peace Corps in Palomar, over in the valley."

Josh's eyes swept down her body from the hat t⌐ ⌐e black flat-heeled shoes. So the woman who caught his eye in the market wasn't a Mamara Indian; she was a Peace Corps volunteer gone native who wanted to borrow money for silver jewelry or a ticket home. He didn't know whether to be disappointed or relieved.

She held out her hand. "Catherine Logan, agricultural specialist."

He shook her hand and felt the calluses on her palm. He thought he could smell fresh fruit, ripening on the trees, but it was the clean scent of her hair and her skin reminding him of summer days and country roads.

He was still holding her hand, and she looked up inquiringly until he realized she was waiting for him to introduce himself.

"Josh Bentley, assistant vice president."

She nodded. "Then I have come to the right place." She sat down again, as if she hadn't heard him say that the answer was no. "I'm working with the villagers to develop a new strain of potatoes, one that takes up less space and produces a higher yield in a shorter time."

Her eyes glowed, and he felt light-headed again. They said it took months before the altitude sickness disappeared for good. He folded his arms across his chest. "How is it working out?'' he asked, watching her lips move as she spoke, still in semishock to find she was an American.

"Fine. Wonderful. Better than I hoped. I'd only done it on the experimental plot at the university, never on a big scale. I'm very excited about it.''

He smiled. "I can see that.''

She leaned forward and drew her eyebrows together. "Can you? Do you mean I've stumbled across the one banker in the world who understands why we need to borrow money to buy a truck to haul our own produce to market?''

Josh rubbed his forehead. He didn't seem to be able to think straight. He didn't know how to explain that he couldn't lend her the money, although he understood why she needed it. But he'd been sent here specifically to put a lid on lending, to put a stop to the making of bad loans.

"Look, Catherine Logan, understanding your need and being able to do something about it are two different things.''

She stood up and stared at him. "You mean the answer is still no?''

He put his hand on her arm. "Do you know there's an international debt crisis and that inflation in Aruaca is running about two hundred percent? Have you heard that every time a borrower defaults on a loan the rate goes up and then poor peasants can't buy shoes or potatoes or—''

She pulled back and squared her shoulders. "Thanks for the lecture. I won't waste any more of your time, since I see your mind was made up before I got here.'' She pressed her lips together. "I should have known. You bankers have an answer for everything. And the answer is always no.''

Josh watched helplessly while she blinked back tears and walked to the door.

"Wait a minute,'' he said, following her across the room. "That's not a fair assessment.''

She grasped the doorknob tightly. "That's not fair? I'll tell you what's not fair. Foreclosing on a family farm after a lifetime of planting and living and—'' She pushed the door open without finishing her sentence and walked out through the reception area to the elevator while he watched.

What had set her off like that? He could understand why she would be disappointed, but to cry over the plight of the family farm seemed like an overreaction. But she wasn't the only one to overreact. Why did he feel such a sense of loss as he stared out the window into the street below, trying to catch a glimpse of a bowler hat and a tear-streaked face?

Dusk fell over the city and lights began to appear across town. The telephone finally stopped ringing. If he hadn't turned the Logan woman down, she would still be sitting in the chair across from his desk, her dark eyes brimming with warmth instead of tears. She would have leaned back and told him in her lilting voice why she had joined the Peace Corps and how she had learned to speak perfect Spanish.

But he'd had no choice. The Aruacan economy was in terrible shape. He was there to tell the people to tighten their belts, not to buy new equipment. But if he couldn't even explain it to a woman with a degree in agriculture, how could he get it across to the man in the street, the people down there hurrying home from work to a meager dinner of beans and rice?

Actually beans and rice didn't sound so bad, he thought, if you had someone to share it with. He wondered where Catherine Logan was right now. How would she get back to Palomar at this time of day? Or was she still down there in the city alone somewhere, carrying a grudge against him as she carried the *ahuayo* on her back?

There was a knock on his door, and his secretary stuck her head in to remind him he had a meeting at 5:00. He walked down the hall to the conference room, and soon he was describing his plan to reduce imports. But his mind continued down another track, a track that led to a farm in a valley where a woman grew potatoes but had no way to get them to town.

There was enough money represented in that room to fund a whole fleet of trucks. If he asked, they would probably agree to make a charitable donation to the agricultural sector. He wouldn't ask them until he asked her if she'd take a truck as a gift. He could picture the look on her face. Joy, wonder, gratitude. He smiled with satisfaction, and the meeting was adjourned.

* * *

Catherine didn't tell the women of the village she didn't get the loan. They didn't even know she had gone to ask for it. That way they wouldn't have to share her disappointment. Or her anger. Or her humiliation at being turned down.

Doña Jacinda took her aside one day as they walked in from the fields, the golden sunshine at their backs, baskets of parsley on their heads, Jacinda's grandchildren trailing behind, munching on carrots. "Tell me, *chiquita*, what is troubling you. You have not been yourself since you returned from La Luz last week."

Catherine steadied the basket on her head. "I'm a country girl," she said. "The city doesn't agree with me. And..." She sighed. "I must go again next week for a meeting and a party to celebrate our Independence Day."

Doña Jacinda clapped her hands together. "A party is just what you need to cheer you up. On our Independence Day there is dancing in the streets. When I was your age, I could dance all night and still work in the fields all day."

Catherine turned to look at the older woman. "How did you manage to do that? When you were my age, you were married with half a dozen children."

Jacinda chewed thoughtfully on a stalk of parsley. "Did I say that?"

Catherine smiled. "I'll never be half the woman you are, *Doñacita*." They reached the small house of Doña Jacinda and set their baskets on a shelf in the hut behind the house.

"How is it that you are not married, Catalina? What is wrong with the men in your country?" The wrinkles in her forehead deepened as her dark eyes probed for the answer.

Catherine leaned against the rack used for drying herbs and fruits. "I don't know any men, Jacinda. I only know boys. And I feel too old for them. Sometimes I feel about one hundred years old."

Jacinda tilted her head to one side and surveyed Catherine carefully. "You are old, that is true, though not quite one hundred. But I am older still and experienced in the ways of the heart. Have I not outlived three husbands already? I saw the look in your eye at the market the other day, and I felt the electricity in the air when you sold the tall man the mangoes. Do you deny you felt something?''

Catherine felt a flush creep up her face and bent over the baskets of parsley to inspect them. ''I don't know who you're talking about, *Doña*.''

Jacinda smiled knowingly. ''Of course not. There have been so many men buying mangoes, how could you remember this one? But I tell you if I had been thirty years younger, I wouldn't have let him get away. You heard that he works in a bank. I have never been in a bank, but I think they may have more money than I have ever seen.''

Catherine looked up. ''Never been in a bank? Never cashed a check or had a bank book?''

Jacinda shrugged. ''No.''

Catherine looked at her thoughtfully. ''You're a farmer, yes. But you're a businesswoman, too, and you need a bank. One day you and I will go together.''

Jacinda's eyes flashed. ''And we will find the man in the suit, the one you don't remember.''

Catherine smiled and ducked under the hanging bouquets of sage and rosemary and waved goodbye. The woman was uncanny. Matchmaker, homemaker, mother and farmer and businesswoman. How could she have felt the vibrations in the air when Catherine herself was doing her best to ignore them? Thank God she hadn't confided in Jacinda about the truck. Let her think the tall stranger was a rich, generous banker. She would never know that the man who caused the electricity in the air was the one who stood between them and the truck they needed.

Let Jacinda hang on to her illusions. Catherine had none left.

Chapter Two

On the Fourth of July the American flag fluttered against a clear blue sky high above the embassy. By the time Catherine arrived, a softball game was in progress behind the main residence and cheers filled the air. The smell of hot dogs sizzling on an outdoor grill lured her through the crowd toward tables festooned with red, white and blue streamers and laden with crisp salads and fresh fruit. She accepted a glass of champagne from a waiter and stepped back to admire an enormous ice sculpture of a swan in the middle of the table.

"Just like home," a deep voice observed dryly from over Catherine's shoulder. She tightened the grip on her glass. She didn't have to turn around to know that the voice belonged to Josh Bentley. She could pretend she didn't hear him and walk away, but she turned and looked. He wasn't wearing his three-piece banker's suit. He was wearing tan slacks and a blue polo shirt that somehow erased the image of the stuffy banker she'd been harboring in her mind. It didn't change the fact that he *was* a stuffy banker, she reminded herself sternly; he just didn't look like one.

So much for avoiding the one person she had come here to avoid. She'd barely arrived and here she was staring at him, wondering if it was just the clothes that made him look more accessible, or the atmosphere or the way his eyes darkened to match the color of his shirt. Like a chameleon.

She was working up her nerve to ask him again for a loan. She would have to humble herself, but for a truck, for the village . . . it was worth it.

"Not like my home," she said lightly. "We don't go in for ice sculptures in Tranquility. Especially on the Fourth of July. It's about a hundred degrees this time of year."

"Tranquility," he repeated, his eyes taking in her sandals, her denim skirt and the contours of her T-shirt.

"Have you heard of it?" she asked incredulously.

He shook his head and rocked back on his heels, then reached for a glass of champagne from a passing waiter. "Could we sit down somewhere and talk? I had an idea after you left my office the other day." He was rewarded with a tentative smile that encouraged him all out of proportion to the situation. He didn't tell her that he had a lot of ideas after she left his office, and most of them had nothing to do with the truck.

With his hand resting lightly on her back they threaded their way through crowds of American expatriots in bright shirts and shorts to a table under a drooping willow tree. She sat in a white lawn chair and looked up at him, her lips parted slightly, her eyes wide and curious. She had unbraided her hair today, and it curled and waved around her face in a dark cloud.

"Is it about the truck?" she asked. "Did you change your mind? Did you decide that one small loan to a group of farm women wouldn't raise the rate of inflation significantly?"

"No. But I think I can get the money for you in another way. In the form of a contribution. It's better than a loan. You won't have to pay it back. It would be a gift."

"A gift? They don't need a gift. They need a loan. They want to be part of the real world. Where people borrow money and pay it back. I want them to feel comfortable walking into a bank and knowing what to do. Writing checks and balancing an account. I know they can do it if someone will give them a chance. A small loan, just enough to buy a truck. They need the truck, but even more they need to be a part of the system.''

He was startled. He'd expected a smile that would light up the embassy grounds, or tears of gratitude. But she sat stiffly in her chair, her hands in her lap.

"It seemed like a good idea . . . at the time," he said evenly.

"It was kind of you to think of it, or whoever thought of it, but the women would never accept such a gift. They're too proud. Once I gave them a pair of old tennis shoes and they gave me a beautiful handwoven shawl. How could they reciprocate if someone gave them a truck?"

He stood and crossed his arms. "They wouldn't have to reciprocate. I can't believe they're too proud to accept something they need so badly."

She nodded firmly. "The worst thing for a Mamara Indian is to feel destitute, and that's what charity does to them. It sends a message that they can't provide for themselves. They begin to lose their self-esteem. The people here are proud, and I have no intention of seeing their pride destroyed by some well-meaning charity. As much as they need a truck, they need their self-respect more. So thanks but no thanks." She stood and glanced around as if she were looking for a place to escape his misguided attempt at philanthropy.

Josh couldn't move. He felt as if he'd had the wind knocked out of him. He was angry. If he'd acted wrongly, it was because he was trying to help. She had no right to make him feel guilty. What right did this do-gooder have to give him a lesson in psychology?

"Wait just a minute," he said, getting out of his chair.

She looked startled, as if a statue had spoken. She obviously thought the conversation was over, but Josh was having none of it. He took her arm to keep her from walking away.

"Look, Ms. Logan, you may be the world's potato expert, and I'll grant you you've been here longer than I have, but I don't think you have a lock on the ethics of the Mamara Indians. I came to Aruaca not only because they requested some help straightening out things at the bank, but because I was interested in the country and the people. It's not an easy job because of the economic problems and the poverty and the inflation, but I'm doing my best."

Her dark eyes widened, her lips pressed together tightly. He couldn't tell what she was thinking. He didn't tell her he'd been requested by banks in Panama and Colombia, but that he'd held out for Aruaca in order to look for a lost silver mine. He hadn't told anyone. They'd think he'd lost his mind. Maybe he had.

"Don't worry," he continued. "I'm not going to bore you with the facts again. I know you think your case is different. Everybody does. Maybe you can grow enough potatoes to pay back your loan. But I don't think so. And over the years I've gotten pretty good at predicting."

"So that's why you're here. Because you're good at saying no."

He dropped his hand from her arm. "That's not the only reason. I've been thinking about coming here long before I was even a banker."

She gave him a thoughtful look from under her dark lashes. "Have you ever made a mistake?"

"Of course I've made mistakes. Bankers are human, too."

Her eyes narrowed. "I've never heard one admit it before."

"What did bankers ever do to you?" he asked, surprised at the bitterness in her voice. "Was it your farm they foreclosed on?"

"That's ancient history," she said brusquely. "Getting back to the loan, before you make your final decision—"

"I have made my final decision. No farm loans this year."

She continued as if he hadn't spoken. "You should really come to the valley. If you could see what we do with so little, I'm sure you'd agree—"

He shook his head and smiled in spite of himself at her determination. "You never give up, do you? Sit down and I'll get you a hot dog and some more champagne."

He waited to see if she really would sit down before he made his way to the grill where he speared two hot dogs, put them in buns and covered them with relish, onions, mustard and catsup. He wouldn't mind going to the valley. In fact, he'd love the chance to get out of the city, but he had no intention of loaning this idealistic Peace Corps volunteer a cent. What would they say back in Boston? What they were already saying here. The altitude's got you, Bentley. Or is it the woman, Bentley? The one who looks like a picture out of the *National Geographic* one day with her pink cheeks and four layers of clothes and the next day she's Miss America in a T-shirt and hip-hugging skirt.

That wouldn't be why you're considering going to the valley, would it? he asked himself. Because if it is, you've got to get back to sea level quick. This woman is interested in one thing, and that's getting a loan. What she isn't interested in is bankers. Unless they shell out, that is. And the minute she realizes you mean it when you say no, she's going to drop you like a hot potato, one of those hybrid potatoes of hers.

He returned to Catherine, balancing two plates of food and two glasses of champagne. He wasn't going to let himself get carried away by her dark, fascinating eyes and the luscious curves under her white shirt and denim skirt. She looked glad to see him, but even gladder to see the potato salad and the hot dog. He sat down across from her again and raised his glass.

"Happy Independence Day."

She lifted her glass and met his gaze. She saw no animosity in his eyes, only warmth and friendliness. He held no grudge, even though she'd turned down his offer. So how could she be angry when he'd said no to her? And there they were, two fellow Americans thousands of miles away from home. Instead of passing like ships in the sea of expatriots, why not have a glass of champagne together before they went on their separate ways? It was a natural thing to do.

"First time out of the country on the Fourth of July?" he asked.

"I was in Aruaca last year, but I didn't come to the party. I don't know why. Something about not wanting to hang out with Americans." As soon as she said it, she wished she hadn't. Now he'd think she'd come to the party in order to see Americans, in order to see him. Nothing could be further from the truth. She'd intended to avoid him. But it hadn't worked out that way.

"So what happens in Tranquility on the Fourth when it's a hundred degrees?" he asked, leaning back in his chair and sipping his champagne. Time enough to resist it later, this feeling that his insides were turning to mush. There was something about this woman that made him forget all the problems he'd told her about—the international debt, the rising inflation; and the one he hadn't—the gnawing fear that the stories of a lost silver mine had played too big a part in his decision to come here. If he'd gone to Panama or Colombia when they wanted him, he might be a VP by now.

Sometimes he thought he'd never adjust to this altitude or learn the language. But sitting here on this chair under this tree, he never felt so well adjusted in his life. What the hell, he told himself. It's a holiday. Eat, drink and be merry and say anything that comes into your head. Tomorrow she'll be gone, back to the country, and it's back to reality.

She put her hot dog down on her paper plate and answered his question. "There's a parade in the morning with the high school band."

"Did you play?"

"Drum majorette."

He smiled. A vision of her in a tightly buttoned jacket, short shorts and long legs in boots drifted in front of him. A mass of dark hair under a crisp white cap.

"Do you miss it?" he asked lazily.

"What, baton twirling?"

"No, Tranquility."

"No," she said so emphatically that he set his glass down and looked at her. "I like it here," she explained. "I may never go back. What about you?"

"I think I'm going to like it. But I'm not used to the altitude, and I haven't seen much except the bank and my apartment, which is two blocks away from the bank."

She shook her head disapprovingly. But she had to admit that for someone who was wrapped up in banking and suffered from altitude sickness, he looked remarkably good. So good she was having trouble bringing the conversation back to the loan.

Instead she found herself watching his eyes change from sky- to sea-blue, listening to the sound of his voice and noticing the muscles in his arms. She never knew bankers had muscles. She never knew bankers had feelings, either. It was disturbing. With an effort she brought herself back to the problem at hand. He hadn't said he wouldn't come to the valley. Maybe if she asked him again.

"Sounds like you need to see some more of the country," she suggested pointedly.

"Such as Palomar?"

"Yes, if you're really interested in the country and the people. Come and meet the women and see how hard they work."

"The women? What about the men?"

"The men are off working in the mines. Farming is women's work around here. If they had to depend on the money from the crops, they'd... Well, they wouldn't starve, but they couldn't buy shoes for the children or tools for the farm."

His eyes narrowed against the late-afternoon sun. "Mines?" he asked. "Not silver mines."

She shook her head. "The silver mines closed years ago. Only the old-timers remember them. They mine tin now, the men of the valley. It's dangerous work, but when they come home they bring the wages. Otherwise..." Her voice trailed off. She'd done everything but get down on her knees and beg him to come. And all he did was change the subject. She wiped her hands on the paper napkin in her lap and decided to make a graceful exit while she still had a few ounces of pride left.

"I'd like to come," he said. "But I'm afraid that no matter how much I like it and how hard the people work I'm going to have to turn you down again." His eyes flashed a warning that she ignored.

"Don't worry about me. I can handle it," she said coolly. "Just come with an open mind." Deep down she had a feeling that if Josh Bentley came to Palomar and met Jacinda and saw how hard everyone worked and how little they earned, he would change his mind. He was a banker, yes, but he also seemed to be a decent human being.

"How about this weekend?" he asked.

Catherine shrugged casually, but her stomach did a flip-flop. She'd done it. Somehow she'd convinced him to come. "Fine," she said.

She stood up. She had a desperate need to get away from his penetrating eyes and his questions. She had already talked too much about herself. She was here to forget about Tranquility, not dredge up memories of happier times, of parades and holidays.

"I have to leave now if I want to catch my ride home."

He stood and looked up at the sky. "You'll miss the fireworks."

"I think I've had enough Americana for one day," she said lightly. "At midnight I turn into a farmer again, and suddenly I'm wearing overalls and a bandanna around my neck."

He reached out and wound his finger around a strand of her hair. "Like Cinderella," he said softly. His face was very close to hers, and she realized that the other guests had drifted away and they were alone under the branches of the tree. If she lifted her face to his, and if their lips met in a brief kiss, no one would know or see.

"Don't run away," he said, his voice so low she had to lean closer to hear him. So close she could feel his breath on her lips. She closed her eyes and felt her spine tingle in anticipation. "You might lose a glass slipper."

Catherine pulled away. He wasn't going to kiss her. He was toying with her. She looked at her watch. "Where has the time gone? I've got to hurry."

"What about this weekend?" he asked.

"I'll expect you Sunday morning."

"How will I find you?"

"Once you get to Palomar, ask anyone where the North American lives."

"I'm not promising anything," he called through the falling shadows.

"Neither am I," she answered over her shoulder, and then she was gone.

Josh stood alone in the dusk, feeling as if he'd lost something he'd been looking for for a long time. He had come that close to kissing her, to feeling her lips on his. She was beautiful, but there was something lurking in the depths of her eyes that kept him at arm's length. He walked slowly through the grounds to the front gate, feeling a pang of something between lonely and homesick. And yet it was neither of those. It was a longing for something he wanted but couldn't have.

Sunday morning dawned clear and hot. Catherine leaned out the bedroom window of her small house and sniffed the air heavy with the scent of the roses that climbed the trellis in her yard. Fertile fields stretched as far as she could see until the hills rose gently in the distance. Farmers had no weekends and this was no exception. She dressed quickly in bib overalls and a checkered shirt and paused in front of the mirror to brush her hair. Suddenly she remembered the feeling of Josh's hand in her hair. Resolutely she braided it as tightly as she could.

He was coming to see the farm, not her. If he came at all. She knotted a ribbon at the end of the braid. The hairstyle was part of her new identity. Along with the skirts and shawls. But no shawl today. It was too hot.

As she walked down the path toward the potato fields, she wondered if she should mention Josh's visit to Jacinda or anyone else. If she told them he was a banker who might lend them money, then she was setting them up for disappointment, but if she didn't tell them, they'd think he was coming to see her. She decided not to worry about it. He might not come at all. But there was something in the air today, a hushed, expectant feeling that something was going to happen. At the edge of the field she bent over to examine the seedlings she had planted a few weeks ago.

"Come on," she coaxed, brushing the dirt off a leaf. "Let's see some progress here. Higher. Reach up and touch the sky." She raised her voice to include the entire field, then stood on tiptoe and spread her arms to demonstrate the technique to the budding potato plants.

Hearing footsteps, she whirled around like a dancer with arms outstretched. There he was in faded jeans and a plaid shirt rolled above the elbows. She dropped her arms and watched him approach, knowing he'd seen her pirouetting among the plants, hoping he hadn't heard her talking to them.

In seconds he was at her side, grinning at her. "Don't let me interrupt. You were saying?"

She blushed. "It's a well-known method, talking to plants. They need encouragement just like people."

He folded his arms across his chest. "Does it work?"

"If you're sincere." She studied him, looking for some sign of sincerity on his part. Did he really want to see the farm? He'd caught her talking to the plants, which put her on the defensive. Now she had to show him how seriously she took her job.

"These are the experimental potatoes I was telling you about." She paused. "The day I came to your office to ask for the loan."

"Oh, yes. The ones that take up less space and produce a higher yield in a shorter time."

She nodded. He did remember. He bent over to rub some soil between his fingers. She knelt down next to him and sunk her hands into the loose, rich earth.

"Look at this. Isn't it beautiful? I wish I could take credit for these potatoes, but anything will grow here. Put a twig in the earth, and the next week you've got a rosebush. Throw an apple core out the window, and the next year there's a tree. What we wouldn't give for two feet of this stuff in California."

His knees next to hers in the dirt, he turned to face her. "So that's where Tranquility is."

"It's in the Central Valley," she explained. "You won't find it on a map of the world." She stood and walked slowly, looking for aphids between rows of plants.

"Is that why you left—to find better soil?" he asked.

"Yes. We had a drought back home for the past three years. And I'd learned a lot I wanted to try out. But we lost our farm. There was nothing to stay for."

"No one to stay for, either?"

"No one," she said firmly. "Do you always interview your loan applicants so thoroughly?" she asked with her hands on her hips.

"It always helps to know their background." He walked on ahead between rows of plants, then stood with his feet wide apart in the rich black earth and looked up at the cloudless blue sky. Sun shone on his strong features. She studied the shape of his nose, his firm jaw and his mouth, remembering that he'd almost kissed her once on the Fourth of July.

"And you," she said, "what made you want to be a banker?"

He paused only a second. "Money and security. Both of which were in short supply when I was growing up. My father was a jack-of-all-trades, and he failed at most of them. He was always looking for something. Unfortunately he never found it. I knew there had to be a better way to support a family."

A family? Catherine's mind reeled. She had never considered the possibility that Josh had a family to support. But, in fact, many families stayed home rather than adjust to the altitude and the language. She walked toward him slowly, her eyes on the plants.

"How is your family?" she asked. What she really meant was who are they and where are they? The words were on the tip of her tongue: are you married?

"My father died in a plane crash a few years ago," he said.

"I'm sorry." She dug a hole in the soil with the toe of her shoe.

"Don't be. It was the way he wanted to go. He didn't want to die in bed. He'd done more living in seventy years than most people do in two lifetimes. He had the most incredible stories to tell ... when he was home, that is." There was sadness and bitterness in his voice.

"Which wasn't very often?"

"No. My mother went to work and I went to school. My father went to look for lost treasure. My mother's family never forgave him."

"Did you?" she asked softly.

He gave her a long look, then shrugged without answering, as if it weren't important. But somehow Catherine knew it was.

Abruptly he changed the subject. "I can just picture your childhood. Jumping into haystacks and raising kittens in the barn."

She studied his face, watched the taut muscles in his neck relax. "That's right, and even though we weren't rich, we never

felt poor. There's always enough to eat on a farm, and my
mother sewed all my clothes. It never occurred to me that I
wouldn't be there forever, making clothes for my children,
canning peaches in the summer and spinning wool in the win-
ter..." She stopped and forced a smile. "Well, let's get going. There's so much I want you to see."

They walked in silence past fields of wheat, a plot of tomatoes ripening in the sun and then the lush green of parsley.
The colors seemed more intense today, the air sweeter and the
earth more fertile. Catherine didn't know if it had anything to
do with the man who walked behind her. Absently she waved
to Doña Blanca, who was guiding a horse pulling a plow across
the field, and the two little boys riding a burro behind her.

Josh nodded to the woman and waved to the children. Then
he turned his gaze back to Catherine, who took the lead down
the narrow path, following her easy gait with his eyes on her
firm, round bottom. He reminded himself he was here on bank
business. Although he could have told her no without coming
all this way. In fact, he did tell her no. Now that he was here he
was more convinced than ever they had no chance of paying
off a loan with their primitive farming methods.

The most he could expect out of today's trip was to convince her to accept the truck as a gift, then convince someone
to give her one. If she wouldn't take it, maybe one of the other
women would, one who wasn't so proud. Like the one who
was waving to them from the doorway of her house.

Catherine introduced Doña Jacinda to him, and she ushered
them into her plain, spotless house. A small boy peeked
through the window, and Jacinda shooed him away. "They are
curious," she said to Josh, "about you." Then she poured
coffee and stood back to survey Josh as if he were the answer
to her prayers. Her gaze traveled to Catherine and back to him,
her rapid Spanish too fast for him to follow. He looked inquiringly at Catherine, seated next to him in a hand-carved
wooden chair.

"She says she remembers you," Catherine said. "From the
market."

"Tell her I remember her, too. Does she know why I'm
here?"

"I haven't told anyone about the loan. So she's jumped to her own conclusions." Catherine set her coffee cup on a small table. "When a man comes calling on a woman in Aruaca, it's for only one reason." Catherine shifted uncomfortably. "So she wants to ask you some questions."

Josh's blue eyes gleamed in amusement. "Fire away."

"She wants to know if you can support a wife." A flush crept up Catherine's face.

"A wife and children, too," he assured her politely.

Catherine translated and waited for the next question. "How many?"

"Four, five, six…as many as possible. I was an only child. Let me tell you, that's no fun at all."

Hearing this, Jacinda raised her palms to the sky and praised God for sending this man to them just in the nick of time. Catherine seemed to have no intention of translating any longer, but Josh caught the drift of what she was saying. Explaining to Jacinda that she wanted to show Josh the farm now, Catherine stood and moved toward the door.

Jacinda insisted that it was too far to walk on such a hot day and brought a placid workhorse around from behind the house for them to ride. Josh made a stirrup with his hands and boosted Catherine onto the horse's broad back, then pulled himself up behind her.

He put his hands on her shoulders, the sun shone on his head and everywhere he looked there were rows of orange squash, red peppers and fields of green grass. The air was clear and clean, and he was beginning to understand how terrible it would be to lose a farm, especially one you had grown up on. The horse plodded down the dirt road as Jacinda watched from her doorway, smiling and waving her approval.

"She likes you, in case you didn't notice." Catherine's voice came from over her shoulder.

"She likes you, too," Josh answered. He hoped the farm was big enough so they could ride around all day like this, swaying back and forth together with the sweet smell of her hair invading his senses.

"She likes me, but she doesn't approve of me roaming the world without a husband. She wants me to get married before it's too late."

Josh moved forward to support her back with his chest. "Do you have anything against getting married?" he asked, his lips so close he could lift her braid and kiss the back of her neck.

"Nothing at all." She inched forward to pat the horse between the ears and break the contact between them. "Just that I'm only interested in the kind that lasts forever. And that's rare, in case you haven't noticed. Take my sister who got married so she could move to town and get off the farm. She's divorced now with two kids. And then Jacinda who's always on my case. She's been married three times, all miners and every one was arranged. It's not her fault that she's outlived them all. But I can't make her understand that I'm just as self-sufficient as she is. And I've got plans that will keep me busy for the next five years. The funny thing is that I came here to help them with all my theories and my hybrid potato stock. But do you know what's happened? I've learned more from them than in four years of agriculture school."

He ran his hand lightly along her shoulder blades, fighting a nearly uncontrollable urge to loosen the braid to see her hair tumble down her back. Her shoulders trembled, and she dug her heels in and urged the horse forward.

"So you can see why I want to do something for them," she said deliberately, "and leave something behind when I go."

He tensed. "The truck?"

"Yes."

"Then let me find a donor for you."

She turned the horse toward a grove of mango trees. "You don't understand. You think that will solve all our problems. But the truck is only part of it. The rest is learning what it means to take out a loan and pay it back. Accepting the responsibility is the big thing, that and the nitty-gritty, writing their names on checks, filling out deposit slips. That's where you come in."

"Catherine…" he began. How was he going to tell her again that the answer was no?

She twisted around on the horse's broad, bare back and pressed her hand against his mouth so he couldn't speak. He wanted to kiss her fingers, one by one, but she turned around quickly before he could do more than think about it.

"Don't make up your mind yet," she said. "You just got here."

The horse stopped under a tree, and she slid to the ground, then stood looking up at him, her dark eyes pleading for his help. She held her hand out to help him down. He took her hand, jumped off and pulled her into his arms, holding her so tightly he could feel her heart beating against his chest. She felt the way he knew she would—warm and soft and desirable.

With one hand he reached behind her and untied the ribbon that held her braid together, and her hair fell in waves, releasing the fragrance of summer flowers. Their eyes met, and for a long moment the only sound was the birds in the branches of the trees overhead.

Finally she stumbled backward and leaned against the tree, her hands clasped behind her back. There was a slight tremor in her voice when she spoke. "I told you I'd do anything to help the people of this valley, but I didn't mean . . ."

"I know you didn't. I was just trying to change your mind about bankers."

"There's only one way you can do that," she insisted.

He came toward her, his eyes a deep, penetrating blue and trapped her against the tree, his hands on either side of her shoulders. "Why are you being so stubborn about this loan? When you have a loan, you're under a lot of pressure. What if something goes wrong, locusts or a flood, and you can't make your payments?" He leaned forward, but she didn't flinch under his gaze.

"Then you'd take back your truck," she answered. "We don't lose anything. And you keep the truck."

"Have you ever tried to sell a used truck?" he asked.

"No, but I'm willing to try." She ducked under his arm, trying to push away the hair that framed her face. "Let's go back to the house," she suggested stiffly.

This time Catherine sat behind Josh, being very careful not to touch him. She looked off to the mountains in the dis-

tance, but his broad shoulders, the shape of his head and the
way his hair grew on the back of his neck made it impossible
for her to concentrate on anything but the man in front of her.
This attraction she felt for him was a problem she had to deal
with. Stubborn, he called her. Yes, she was stubborn. And
determined to keep their relationship all business.

Catherine tied the horse in front of her house. A delicious
smell wafted through the open windows from the kitchen and
she gave Josh a puzzled look. In the oven they found a *torta*
made of fresh eggs and layered with herbs and cheese. On the
table there was a loaf of Jacinda's wheat bread and a bottle of
country wine. Catherine smiled to herself. Jacinda was pulling out all the stops, convinced that the way to a man's heart
was through his stomach.

The heat from the wood-burning stove had turned the small
house into an oven, and Catherine suggested they carry the
table outside to the shade. Hungry and hot and tired, they ate
in silence, refilling their glass tumblers with the dark, cool wine
and looking at each other warily between bites.

By the time the torta plate was empty, half a loaf of bread
gone and the wine bottle drained, Josh was eyeing the hammock stretched between two willow trees. He yawned lazily.
"I've been up since 5:00," he explained.

"So have I," she countered.

"No siesta for farmers?" he inquired.

She shook her head. The heat and the wine and the sun
made her long to stretch out in her hammock, too, and swing
in the breeze. But she couldn't relax with Josh Bentley around.
If she did, he would talk her out of the loan. If she let her de-
fenses down for one minute, he could sweep away her reasons
like dust on the road. Of course, she was worried about making the payments. She was stubborn, but not stubborn enough
to keep this up much longer.

After clearing the table with brisk efficiency, Catherine led
Josh on a thoroughly businesslike tour of the remaining sixty
acres of farmland, from the root cellars to the orchard and
chicken coop. She introduced him to all the women and children who paused in their work to look him over and smile
broadly. As they passed, the people pressed gifts on Josh un-

til he was loaded down with a sack of fresh vegetables, jars of honey and pounds of homemade cheese by the time they returned to Catherine's small house.

Jacinda appeared on cue at the front porch as they jumped off her draft horse. Catherine assured her she would feed and water the horse and bring him back later. She was hot and tired and frustrated. She was going to ask him one more time, but she knew what he was going to say. She had sensed it all afternoon. She felt it from the way he kept his eyes on the fields and from the questions he asked. From the cool brush of his hand when he helped her off the horse.

But Jacinda lingered, suggesting she bring over a fresh chicken for their dinner. Catherine gave her a look that said there would be no "their" dinner, but Jacinda only shrugged and said she'd be back a little later. Catherine looked pointedly at Josh's car parked out at the road, and he followed her gaze.

"I've enjoyed the day," he said slowly. "I'm just sorry..."

"Sorry you can't lend us the money? Don't worry. I understand. I understand that bankers will only bet on a sure thing. For a while I hoped you were different. I thought you were different, but I see you're just like all the others. Cautious, even though we're talking about one measly truck. Surely that's only small change for a big bank like yours. Why can't you take a chance for once in your life? What have you got to lose?"

"I told you..."

"If something happens and we can't make the payments, the truck is yours. I'll deliver it to you personally. Then I'll help you resell it."

"It's not as simple as that." Josh frowned. "I shouldn't have come. I didn't know you were counting so much on it."

"I wasn't," she insisted. It was true. She hadn't counted on it. She had only hoped. And once again her hopes had been dashed. Once again by a banker. She picked up his bags and packages and unceremoniously loaded them in his arms. His mouth set in a tight line, he said goodbye and walked to his car.

Chapter Three

It was when he dumped the bags of food in the back seat of the car that he saw the thin stream of greenish liquid running down the road and forming a pool in a pothole. He exhaled loudly and cast a quick look back at the house. Catherine was nowhere in sight. She had made it clear she didn't want to see him again. He thought she'd want to see him drive away, though, just to have the satisfaction of knowing he'd really gone.

He lay down under the car on the hot pavement, feeling the heat burn through his shirt and jeans, and confirmed what he already knew. The origin of the greenish liquid was the radiator of his car. He swore loudly in the late-afternoon silence, stood up and looked under the hood. The radiator was bone dry. He walked back to the house and knocked on her front door.

The sound of water running came from somewhere in the house. So at least she had running water, though she cooked on a wood stove and had no electricity that he noticed. Was she washing dishes or herself? He pictured her in the shower with rivulets of water running down her breasts, and the heat rose in his body from the soles of his shoes to the top of his head.

He sat down on the front porch and chewed on a stalk of grass to calm down. When the water stopped, he stood and knocked again. Silence.

"Hello," he called loudly. "I'm sorry to bother you, but I need to borrow a cup of water for my radiator."

Her muffled voice came from somewhere in the house. "Just a minute."

She came to the door, wearing a large white towel wrapped around her body. In her hand she held a metal cup filled with water, which she gave him without a word. Maybe she thought it was a trick so he wouldn't have to leave.

"I'll be right back," he assured her, trying not to notice the full curves under the terry cloth. He turned quickly and walked back to his car. When he poured the water into the radiator, it dribbled out through a crack in a rubber hose. He swore under his breath this time, just in case she was still at the door, listening. He should have realized that at this altitude water had reached the boiling point somewhere between La Luz and Palomar and split the hose. All perfectly understandable. What he didn't understand was why it had to happen today.

He sat down on the road in the shadow of the car and stared back at the small house. If he were in a city, he'd call a tow truck and a taxi. He'd buy a new hose and have it installed. But he was in Palomar with no tow truck, no spare parts and, worst of all, no place to get out of the sun.

Although he was within spitting distance of a comfortable house belonging to a fellow American, he might as well be in the middle of the desert for all the good it did him. At least in the desert there was the spirit of hospitality for the traveler. He had already used up his quota of Catherine Logan's hospitality. He supposed he could sleep in a field. And he had plenty of food. He wouldn't starve. If only it weren't so hot. He wiped his forehead and thought about Catherine, still wet and cool from the shower. If he hadn't wasted the cup of water on the radiator, he could have drunk it.

And now he was hallucinating. He thought he saw her on the porch, wearing shorts and a shirt, her hands on her hips. He stood up, blinked and looked again. She was real. She was moving her lips.

"What are you doing out there?" she called.

He walked slowly back to the house, the empty cup in his hand. "There's a little problem with my car," he said grimly. "I was wondering if I could use your telephone."

She looked surprised. "Who are you going to call?"

"A garage."

She shook her head. "Even if I had a telephone, you couldn't call a garage because they aren't open on Sunday."

"Well, then a tow truck."

"Get real, Bentley. There is no garage. There is no tow truck within a hundred miles. What is it you're looking for?"

"A rubber hose. The one I have is cracked."

"Try La Luz, and if they don't have one, there's always Bogotá."

He nodded slowly. "Well, I won't take any more of your time. You've been more than helpful and I'll be on my way."

"Where are you going?" she asked with an exasperated sigh.

"Back to the city."

"What are you going to do—walk? I hate to disappoint you, but you're stuck here for the night, or half the night. The truck comes to get us at 3:00 a.m. for market. You can ride along if you want and try to buy a hose in town tomorrow. Until then..."

"Don't worry about me," he assured her. "I'll just camp out in my car. I've got plenty of food."

Her eyes took in his perspiring face, his damp shirt and his grim expression.

"Why don't you come in for another glass of water?" she asked, tucking a wet curl behind her ear.

"Thank you," he said, following her into the kitchen. "I gave the last one to my radiator."

She watched him drain the glass she gave him and set it in the sink. He stood and looked at her, watching her run her hand through the tangle of damp curls. The fragrance of hand-milled soap filled the air. His gaze slid down to her bare feet and then up her legs. A smattering of freckles across her knees surprised him. He felt the muscles in his abdomen tighten, and he realized he was in dangerous territory, emotionally and physically. He had to get out of there before he made a complete fool of himself. Just as he was turning to leave, she spoke.

"If you don't mind a cold shower, you can use mine. I'm afraid I used up all the hot water, but . . ."

"A cold shower is exactly what I need," he said.

She showed him to a stall made of corrugated plastic tacked on to the house as an afterthought, and then she disappeared. The water was cold and clear and pumped in from the well in the backyard. The tank backed into the chimney, allowing water to be heated by the fire. The soap was her soap. He stood there and let the water run through his hair and down his face, and he wished to hell she would take the truck as a gift and they could be friends. He had a feeling she was as proud as the Indian women. Too proud to accept charity. He understood that. Growing up poor could do that to you.

The other thing he wished was that he could get into his car and drive back to La Luz. Even as he dried off with her towel, he knew the shower hadn't solved his problem. He was filled with an intense desire for a woman who hated all bankers and him in particular and was only interested in what he could do for her. Now that she knew he wasn't going to give her what she wanted, she was even sorrier than he was that his car had broken down. As soon as he thanked her, he'd go back to his car and wait until the truck came at 3:00. He tried not to think of the car as an inferno, its black surface absorbing the afternoon sun.

Catherine was sitting under a tree behind the house packing raspberries to sell at the market when Josh walked through the back door. She looked up and dropped several berries on the ground. Now that the dirt and dust were gone his strong features stood out in stark relief. His eyes, the color of the late-afternoon sky, held her gaze across the yard. Just when she was prepared to let him spend the night in his car, he came out of her shower looking at home, as if he belonged there, too.

Carefully she picked up the berries and resumed her packing. Casually she said, "Jacinda was here. She brought a chicken for dinner."

"Your dinner," he said.

"Your dinner, too. She made that quite clear."

"That was nice of her."

Catherine pushed the boxes aside. "She's afraid I'll let you slip through my fingers. She sees you as my last hope before I dry up and blow away."

Josh leaned against the side of the house, his arms folded across his chest. "No chance of my slipping away today. Why didn't you tell her you have this thing about bankers before she got her hopes up? Didn't you tell her we're all slime bags who foreclose on innocent women and children and take away their homes?"

She stood up with her basket over her arm. "I never said that. I know you're just doing your job. I just wish—"

"You wish it weren't my job. Sometimes I wish it weren't, either. If I were a farmer, you would have kissed me today under the tree, wouldn't you?"

Her eyes widened, and her heart beat out a warning. "Wait a minute. Don't jump to conclusions. I'm not looking for a farmer. I'm not looking for anybody. I admit there may be something between us. I don't understand it, but I don't deny it."

He nodded. "Like lightning bolts. You don't have to understand them to feel them when they hit you."

She swallowed hard. So he felt it, too, the current that flowed between them. It was time to put a stop to this right now, and the best way to do it, other than telling him the truth, was to agree with him.

"You're right, you know. I do have a thing against bankers that goes way back. I can't change it, you can't change it, no matter what you do. Even if you lend us the money. That's why it has to be only business between us. Surely you can see that lending us money is good business. We'll take good care of the truck. We'll make our payments on time. And you'll get a whole lot of new customers." The words were coming faster and faster. She paused to take a breath. "What's wrong with that?"

"Nothing, in theory. But I told you—"

She brushed past him and walked to the back door. "I know what you're going to say. I don't want to hear it again. Let's drop it. We're stuck here together for a few more hours. Then you can go back to banking and I can go back to farming."

Josh felt as if she'd slapped him in the face. "I'm sorry I ruined your day. Is there anything I can do to make it up to you?"

"You can start a fire out back to barbecue the chicken. That way we won't have to heat up the house." She turned and went into the kitchen.

As he tossed branches of apple wood into a pile, he realized she didn't bother to deny that he'd ruined her day. Well, she hadn't done much to make his, either. Except for the lunch, and Jacinda had made that. Then there was the encounter under the mango tree, where he had almost lost his control and she had almost given in to the feelings she tried so hard to hide. Was this really a generic hatred of bankers as she claimed, or was it something else, something he couldn't even guess at?

When she came outside again, the smoke was curling up from the fire. Expertly she threaded the chicken on the spit, and Josh turned the crank until his arm ached and his face was covered with soot. She set the table and brought out a pot of rice and a platter of homegrown tomatoes. Then she poked a fork into the chicken and nodded her approval.

After he washed up, they made polite, impersonal conversation while they ate. But when she wasn't looking he allowed himself some very personal glances—at the neckline of her T-shirt and the line where her shorts met her thighs. As the shadows lengthened, he studied her profile and the way her hair brushed her cheek. When she got up to get the coffee, he realized he would never see her legs again or the freckles on her knees, because tomorrow she would be wearing her market clothes and that would be the end of it. Of everything.

No more would he make a fool of himself hanging around the Rodriguez Market, waiting to see if she'd appear. No more feeble attempts at bargaining. As she had said, she'd go back to farming and he'd go back to banking. Finally. This had been the longest and most frustrating day of his life. And it wasn't over yet.

He stood and walked around the yard. It was almost dark. If it hadn't been for the light from the fire, he wouldn't have noticed the hammock swaying invitingly in the evening breeze. He leaned against the canvas. It was wide, big enough for two. Fat chance, he told himself. Catherine set two cups on the table and a pot of coffee.

"Don't get too comfortable," she cautioned. "That's where I sleep."

He straightened. "Don't worry. I'm just going to stretch out in the back seat of my car. Don't forget to knock on my window in the morning so I won't miss the truck."

"That's not necessary. You can have my bedroom upstairs. It ought to cool off pretty soon. That way I won't have to knock on your window. You'll hear the rooster crow."

"If you're sure . . ."

"I'm sure. I never use it in the summer." She poured a cup of coffee and delivered it to him, determined to be hospitable to the end which, God willing, would be only a few more hours. Then Josh Bentley would disappear from her life. Hopefully an anonymous tow truck would come to get his car, then she would never have to see him again.

After he finished his coffee, she led him to the small bedroom furnished with only a narrow bed and a chest of drawers. She paused long enough to collect her nightgown from a hook on the wall and a blanket from the foot of the bed. In the dim gaslight on the wall the large outline of his body filled the doorway. She stood at the top of the stairs.

"Do you need anything else?" she asked politely.

There was a long silence while she felt rather than saw his eyes on her.

"Do you?"

She shook her head and hurried down to the kitchen where she changed into her nightgown in the dark. Did she need anything else? Good question. He made her want something else, she knew that, and wants were only a hairbreadth from needs. Needs that were as basic as food and water and just as primal. Her skin prickled as the soft cotton slid over her breasts.

Barefoot, she tiptoed out past the dying embers of the fire and lay down in the hammock, her blanket wrapped around her. As she watched, the gaslight in the upstairs window went out. She closed her eyes tightly and willed herself to go to sleep. But she thought of the man in her room, in her bed, and the thought disturbed her more than she imagined. The light in her bedroom went on again. Why didn't he go to sleep? He said he'd been up since 5:00.

There was a thumping sound. The sound of someone coming down the stairs in the dark. Then kitchen sounds. Glass clinking against glass. What was he doing?

"Josh?"

He came to the back door. "I can't sleep. It must be the coffee. I was looking for something to drink." He lifted a glass.

"There's fresh water in the icebox."

He returned to the kitchen, then she saw the outline of his body as he stepped out into the yard, wearing his same clothes, but barefoot, too. He bent his head back and let out an appreciative whistle. "What a view of the southern sky. From my balcony in town it looks like soup."

"Too much peripheral light," she agreed.

"Hey, there's the Southern Cross. I've been here for two weeks, and this is the first time I've seen it."

Catherine stood and wrapped her blanket tightly around her instinctively. "Where is it? I've been here for eighteen months and I still haven't found it."

He came up behind her and put his hands on her shoulders. "That's because it's not really a cross. There's no central star to mark the X. It looks more like a kite."

She felt the warmth of his hands through her blanket as she tilted her head back. She told herself she could see the stars just as well from the comfort of her hammock, but for some reason she stayed right where she was, leaning back against his chest, listening to him point out the brilliant Jewelbox cluster and the dark nebula called Coalsack. His deep voice caused vibrations to echo through her body.

"I've always wanted to see Scorpio," she said in a dreamy voice she scarcely recognized as hers. If he had let her go, she would have fallen over backward. But she knew he wouldn't.

"Actually," he said softly, his lips against her ear, "the hammock is a better place to watch the constellations."

Scorpio flashed her a warning signal from four hundred light-years away.

"For you or for me?" she asked.

"It looks as if it's big enough for two," he suggested as they walked together toward the hammock.

She hesitated. "I don't know. I've never tried it." She looked up for a sign from Scorpio, but he seemed to be urging her on, asking her, "What harm would it do to study the sky for a few minutes?" Telling her it was a wide hammock, large enough for two.

But no matter how strong or how wide the hammock, when Josh settled down next to her, their bodies were pressed together, shoulder to shoulder, hip to hip and thigh to thigh. He crossed his arms under his head and continued his lecture, apparently unaware of the heat waves he was generating in her body. How could he know he had started a chain reaction a few weeks ago in the marketplace that grew stronger and harder to resist every time she saw him?

The sound of his voice describing the location of the South Pole soothed her, and the constellations blurred before her eyes. She turned onto her side, her back to him. He stopped talking and shifted so that they were back to back. She sighed. She should tell him to leave now and go back upstairs, but it was so hot up there and the air was cool out here. So deliciously cool. And it felt so good to lie there, her back against his. She opened her mouth to tell him . . . what was it she was going to tell him?

"Do you know what?" she whispered.

"No."

"You paid too much for the mangoes." There, she'd gotten it off her mind.

Just before she drifted off to sleep, she felt his hand tousle her hair. "I know," he said, "but it was worth it."

When the rooster crowed, Catherine sighed and buried her head in her blanket. It took a long moment before she realized she wasn't alone. She lay perfectly still, afraid to turn and see if Josh was awake. Maybe if she rolled over the edge of the hammock and onto the ground, she could pretend she really hadn't spent the night as close to Josh Bentley as a person could get. Well, almost as close.

But just as she moved her leg over the side, she felt him shift his weight and drop one arm over her shoulders. She twisted around to face him. In the darkness she saw that his eyes were closed. The shadow of a dark beard grazed his face. A slight smile played at the corner of his mouth. He was breathing deeply. Still asleep.

She felt her muscles relax as she unconsciously matched his breathing with her own, mesmerized by the rise and fall of his chest. What had happened to her plan to slip away? Maybe Jacinda had put something in the wine. Some herb, some magic potion to rob her of her self-control. She wouldn't put it past her. Jacinda was determined to push her into someone's arms. Not just someone's—Josh's.

Before she realized what was happening, Josh tightened his arm around her shoulders and drew her to him, the half smile deepening. Taking a deep breath, she slid out from under his arm and rolled out of the hammock. A low moan escaped his lips, and Catherine looked down at him, her blanket over her shoulders, her hands on her hips.

"It's time to get up," she said firmly, ignoring the sight of his broad chest as he stretched lazily.

He gave her a sleepy smile. "I was in the middle of a dream," he protested.

"Sorry," she said briskly. "No time for dreams. The truck will be here in a few minutes. And I know you're anxious to get to town and get your... whatever it was."

"My hose." He sat on the edge of the hammock and ran his hand through his hair, making it stand on end. His clothes were wrinkled, his face lined with sleep, and she realized that he was still the most attractive man she'd ever seen.

She turned quickly before she said something stupid. "I'm going up to change."

He watched her go, long, slender legs, bare feet hitting the ground as if she were wearing boots. The remnants of the dream clouded his vision. He was holding her in his arms and swaying in a hammock on a tropical beach. The best part was that Catherine wasn't a dream. If anything, she was more beautiful, more bewitching in real life. The worst part was that sleeping next to him had meant nothing to her. He could tell by the look on her face as she had stood there gazing down at him, announcing the arrival of the truck as if he were a passenger in a bus station.

The harsh beep of a horn broke his reverie. A diesel engine clattered in the distance. He walked across the yard and stood under her bedroom window. "Catherine."

She leaned out the window, hair braided, shawl in place, and looked down at him.

"Are my shoes up there?" he asked.

Without speaking she threw them down one at a time, and he caught them in one swift motion. Then, very firmly and deliberately, she shut the window and was gone.

"Thanks," he said loudly to the closed window. Then he washed his face in the kitchen sink, put his shoes on and stood in front of her house. The lights from the truck grew brighter as it came down the hill. At the edge of the road he glared at his useless car. "Traitor," he said loudly. "Deserter. Where were you when I needed you?" Over the whine of the fast-approaching truck he didn't hear her walk up behind him.

"Don't let me interrupt," she said. "You were saying?"

He turned to look at her. A glimmer of humor danced in her dark eyes. "It's a well-known technique talking to cars," he explained dryly. "They need encouragement just like people."

"Well, that didn't sound like encouragement to me."

"What this car needs is a kick in the tires," he explained.

She opened her mouth to reply, but the breaks squealed and the truck pulled up in front of her house. He helped her load the baskets of raspberries into the long flatbed between bags of lettuce and mangoes. The farm women he had met yesterday welcomed him with shrieks of surprise, made room for him in the corner next to Catherine and erupted into a stream of gossip in their Indian language.

He gave Catherine an inquiring look. She smiled at him for the first time since yesterday when he arrived. And with the smile came the first streaks of light across the sky. A new day, filled with new possibilities. With Catherine Logan? Probably not. Probably he'd never see her again. A garage would send a tow truck or a man with the parts. He would never go to the Rodriguez Market again. He would buy his groceries at the supermarket in town. She didn't want to see him. He didn't want to see her. But there was that smile, and the eyes and that look she had that was half farmer's daughter and half exotic gypsy.

"What are they talking about?" he asked.

There was a glint in her eyes. "You and me. They want to know what happened last night. They're very curious, you know."

"Did you tell them?"

"There's nothing to tell. We had dinner, went to bed, got up and that's it." She twisted the fringe on her shawl and avoided his gaze.

"You forgot the astronomy lecture." He slanted her a look, hoping for some reaction, anything. She didn't disappoint him.

Her eyes flashed. "Don't you even hint that we slept together in the hammock. That's the kind of thing that's cause for a shotgun wedding. They don't understand casual... informal..." She faltered. "They wouldn't understand. Trust me."

He reached for her hand and shook it firmly. "I'll trust you if you'll trust me. Now just let me explain the whole thing."

She opened her mouth to protest, but he held up his hand. "Give me a chance," he said, and she pressed her lips together.

He turned to Doña Jacinda. "My car," he began in halting Spanish, "has a problem."

Jacinda threw back her head and laughed loudly. Unperturbed, he continued. "Catalina was kind enough to offer me shelter for the night." At this the whole truckload of women shouted their approval. Catherine's face turned red, and she pulled the brim of her bowler hat down over her eyes.

"What happened?" Josh asked. "I know my Spanish isn't very good, but what did I say?"

She shook her head helplessly. "It doesn't matter what you said. They think they know what happened. Anyway, you've made their day."

He looked around at their smiling faces, listened to their chatter without understanding one word, then leaned against a sack of peppers. "How often do you do this?"

She tilted her hat back, feeling the heat recede from her cheeks at last, grateful for the change of subject. "Twice a week during harvest. We're better off than most of the women you see in the market. We grow our own crops so we keep our own profits. Or we would if..." She paused and looked at the driver.

"If you didn't have to pay the driver. If you had your own truck," he finished for her.

"You said it, I didn't." She gave him a long look. "For every head of lettuce, every mango, every bunch of parsley we sell, he gets half the profits." She tied her shawl in a knot under her chin, choking back her resentment.

"How much does he charge?" Josh asked with a troubled frown.

"It's not what he charges. It's the interest. We don't have the cash to pay him in the morning, and by evening the interest has risen by fifty percent."

His dark eyebrows drew together. "That sounds like usury."

"Of course, but we have no choice. We just hope to break even. They think that's the way it has to be, but I know better. I know you go to the bank in the spring for seed money and in the fall you pay it back." The picture of stern old Mr. Grant floated before her eyes and she paused. "Theoretically," she added.

"You do know what happens if you can't make the payments," he said soberly.

"Of course I know. I've seen farms sold and I've seen divorces and suicides. But we're not talking about mortgaging the farm here. We're talking about a truck, one truck, even one used truck in good shape." She wiped her mouth with the back of her hand. "I'm sorry. I promised I wouldn't talk about it anymore."

The wooden slats that held the produce rattled as the truck rounded a curve, and Catherine fell against Josh's shoulder. She tried to move back to her place, but he put his arm around her waist under her shawl and held her tightly.

"It still hurts to think about your farm, doesn't it?" he asked, his lips against her ear.

"Yes." She didn't want to talk about it, didn't want to think about it, but sometimes it came back to her like a bad dream. Not as often as before, though. These past eighteen months had been good for her. As long as she stayed far away from Tranquility, California, and the States, she could keep the bad dreams at bay.

"Are you sure you want to take a chance again with a loan, with a bank and with a banker?"

She looked around the truck at the women, at their round, honest faces, weathered by the sun, lined with hard work. "Yes, it's worth it. If you never take chances, you're stuck in a rut. If they had a loan..." She bit her lip, determined never to mention it again. She leaned back and closed her eyes, afraid to meet his gaze, afraid to hear him say no again.

Josh stretched his arms along the top of the wooden slats. Taking chances was what bank loans were all about. He'd been a loan officer once. On his way to becoming a vice president. Minimizing risks was the name of the game, and this was a risk that had No written all over it. He reminded himself of the balance of payments, of rising inflation, and all he could think about was the woman next to him, the scent of her hair, the way her body felt pressed next to his and the swaying motion lulling her to sleep.

Was he going to violate every principle of good business just because he was touched by her story? He studied the faces of the women. Or was he going to make a decision based on some cockeyed idea that one truck loan could bring them into the twentieth century?

Take a chance... if you never take chances... The words went around in his brain. His father took chances. His life was made up of one chance after another, and you couldn't say that he was ever stuck in a rut. To him a rut was staying home.

It was taking a job and going to work every day and bringing home a paycheck.

By the time they reached the outskirts of town, Josh was still undecided and Catherine was sleeping with her head on his shoulder. The truck screeched to a halt, and she woke up, her gaze so open, so trusting that he knew he'd do whatever it took to earn that trust, to get them their loan. The driver twisted around in his seat and nodded at him, and the women moved aside so he could step over the produce and jump out.

With a belch of diesel smoke the truck pulled away. He stood on the corner with the small cars and buses rushing by and shoved his hands into his pockets.

"Thanks for the ride," he called, but his words were swallowed up in the cacophony of horns. He watched as the truck turned the corner. She hadn't even said goodbye. He went home to shower and change. He had a big day ahead of him.

In the afternoon the market was filled with masses of people. The mountain air was cool, but the sun was hot, beating down on the corrugated plastic and turning the stall into a sauna. Catherine yawned for the third time and Jacinda beckoned to her.

"Come," she said, removing her apron and settling her hat at a jaunty angle. "I'm going to see my friend Doña Margarita, the weaver. I promised her some of my peppers."

Catherine put her hat on a wooden crate, wiped the perspiration from her forehead and gratefully followed Jacinda up the steeply inclining street. At the top of the hill she gazed in awe at Teregape, one of the most spectacular mountains in the Andes, its white peak visible in the clear afternoon air. The awesome sight lifted her spirits and made her forget for a moment her fatigue and her humiliation at being turned down—again.

Doña Margarita was too busy to admire the beauty of the mountain that towered above her shop. Briefly acknowledging the arrival of her friend Jacinda, she supervised her daughter at the loom and waited on customers. An alpaca sweater dyed a natural rose color hung on a hanger at the entrance to the stall. Rubbing the soft wool between her thumb and forefinger, Catherine caught Jacinda's eye. Jacinda smiled and nodded emphatically.

"It was meant for you, *chica,*" she said. "Perhaps we can trade for eggs or—"

Catherine shook her head. She wouldn't take their produce and use it for barter. It was too precious. She reached into her pocket. "I have money. A birthday present from my mother." She examined the price written on a paper pinned to the hem of the sweater. "It's not expensive."

Jacinda held the sweater up to Catherine's shoulders and nodded her approval. "Leave the bargaining to me," she whispered.

When Margarita finally cleared the stall of customers and turned her attention to Catherine and Jacinda, she sent her daughter to the crate in back to fetch a bolt of handwoven wool. The loosely woven fabric was a mixture of pink and rose and mauve and a perfect match for the pink sweater. Catherine stood still while they wrapped the material around her hips, then pinned and tucked and turned her around like a department store mannequin.

She didn't remember saying yes, but she had no intention of saying no as the women chattered and beamed their approval. While she watched, Margarita's daughter stitched up the side and sewed a waistband around the top. Jacinda and Margarita settled on a price, and Catherine paid and walked out with the first new clothes she'd bought since she'd arrived in Aruaca. The fact that she had no place to wear such a beautiful handmade outfit didn't occur to her until she returned to their stall. Oh, well, she could always send it to her sister for Christmas.

The other women insisted she try on the new clothes, and behind the crates they spread their skirts to give her privacy. Pulling the sweater over her head, Catherine loosened her braid and let her dark hair fall over one shoulder in a mass of waves.

The skirt flared from her hips, then floated to midcalf, the rose-colored sweater caressing her skin above her pink lace bra. She held out her arms, and to the women's delight, twirled around in front of the parsley and melons.

Giddy from lack of sleep, Catherine suddenly realized that shadows were falling over the marketplace. Without taking time to change her clothes she began packing up to go home. She didn't look forward to being in the truck without someone to sleep on. Resolutely she banished the thought from her mind, the thought of strong, broad shoulders and a soothing voice, and picked up her old clothes to change for the ride home.

But out of the corner of her eye, as if she'd made him appear by thinking about him, Josh was approaching. Easily visible above the crowd, he was wearing his three-piece suit, the jacket slung over his shoulder just like the first time she'd seen him. She stood staring at him as the contrast of light and shadow played tricks on her eyes, afraid that if she took her eyes away for even a moment, he would disappear like a mirage.

Their eyes locked and held as he came closer and closer until he finally stood facing her, his eyes taking a tour of her new skirt and sweater. She felt her body respond as if he'd touched her. But he didn't. He only looked. Her skin tingled, her heart pounded until he finally spoke.

"Are you going somewhere?" he asked.

"Yes, home." She followed his gaze. "Oh, you mean because I'm wearing... These are my new clothes I bought from Jacinda's friend the weaver." She was babbling. She couldn't stop.

Jacinda sidled up to Josh. *"¿Le gusta?"* she asked, nodding her head at Catherine.

He smiled. *"Me gusta mucho,"* he assured her, using one of the phrases he was sure of. The Spanish class he'd taken before he'd come occasionally paid off.

Pleased, Jacinda went back to her packing while Catherine's face turned the delicate pink of her sweater.

"I'm glad I caught you," he said. "I owe you a dinner. And I've got some news for you."

She shook her head. "You don't owe me anything. Can't you just tell me the news? The truck will be here in a few minutes." She began piling papayas into boxes with potatoes without knowing what she was doing.

"It'll take longer than a few minutes. It'll take about three hours, about as long as it takes to eat dinner in a restaurant around here." He rocked back on his heels, radiating patience, waiting until she made up her mind.

"Not if you go to the Folklore Club in the city," she said, smoothing the fabric of her new skirt.

"Is that the place that's crowded with Peace Corps volunteers?"

"Yes, it's busy and noisy, but the food is good and cheap."

He shook his head. "That's not where we're going."

"Oh." She was suddenly out of breath and out of fruit and vegetables to pack. The women were starting the trek to the truck, the leftover produce on their backs once again. "How would I get home?" she asked a little desperately.

"Taxi," he answered. "I'm going to go get my car, anyway. I have my new hose in here." He lifted his briefcase, then set it down. "I know what's bothering you. You don't know how to tell Jacinda and the women. I'll handle that."

Openmouthed, she watched him waylay Jacinda as she passed with a stack of empty boxes and explained, augmenting his limited Spanish with sign language, that he was taking *la Catalina* to dinner and would bring her home in a taxi before the rooster crowed.

There was no mistaking Jacinda's approval. The look in her eyes was worth a thousand words. And before she knew it Catherine was being hustled out of the marketplace with Josh's hand firmly on her elbow. Skyscrapers, rising to meet the hills that surrounded the city, cast shadows over the wide streets. Teregape was bathed in a reddish glow.

With the sun sinking behind the altiplano the temperature was dropping, but Catherine didn't notice. She felt the warmth of Josh's hand on her arm. He said he had news. He wouldn't take her out to dinner to give her bad news, would he? Standing there waiting for a break in the steady stream of cars, she didn't know.

She couldn't think. She could only feel, and what she felt was light-headed and short of breath. And after eighteen months she could hardly blame the altitude. It must be something else.

Chapter Four

Stepping off the noisy crowded street and into the Restaurante Roberto was a shock. Suddenly it was calm and quiet. A maître d' in a tuxedo glided forward across a tiled floor and bowed from the waist.

"*Buenas noches, Guillermo,*" Josh said.

Guillermo's eyes flickered over Catherine for a moment, and a faint smile crossed his lips. "Dinner for two, sir?" he asked in heavily accented English.

Josh nodded and placed his hand on Catherine's back. They followed Guillermo past deep leather booths that lined the walls. Sconces holding candles shone on solitary diners and large parties alike. In the far corner they settled into soft leather seats on opposite sides of a quiet booth.

The gilt-tasseled menu lying unopened in front of her, Catherine looked around wide-eyed at the understated elegance of the place. From somewhere on the other side of the room someone was playing an old Rodgers and Hart song on a piano. After lighting the candle on their table, Guillermo slipped discreetly away.

The candlelight flickered on Josh's face. His firm jaw was clean-shaven. He didn't look as if he'd spent the night in a hammock. She smoothed an imaginary wrinkle in her skirt. What if she hadn't bought these clothes? Would Guillermo have signaled his approval if she'd been wearing her bowler hat and shawl? She opened her menu and skimmed the entrées: *crêpes des champignons,* pasta primavera and grilled chateaubriand.

"Oh, just like home," she murmured.

"Not like my home," he said, laugh lines crinkling at the corners of his eyes.

"Do you come here often?" she asked.

"Every night."

Her mouth fell open.

He shrugged. "I feel comfortable here and my stove hasn't arrived yet. When it does . . ."

She waited, fingering the menu.

He smiled. "When it does, I'll probably still eat here every night."

She shook her head in dismay.

"Does that sound boring to you?" he asked.

"A little," she admitted, although looking at him across the table, boring wasn't the word that came to mind. He'd taken his suit coat off, loosened his tie and rolled up his sleeves, exposing suntanned arms from his day in the country. The words that came to mind were strong, sexy and handsome. She tore her eyes away and looked down at the menu again. The prices horrified her. She closed the menu. "I'll let you order," she said, and leaned back against the soft leather. "Don't tell me you have the same thing every night."

He rested his elbows on the table, a glint in his eyes. "I'm not that unimaginative," he protested. When the waiter came, he ordered a Caesar salad, wine from Argentina and two medium rare steaks.

There was a silence and she looked up expectantly. "You said you had news."

"Yes. You can have your truck."

A smile crossed her face and lit her dark eyes, then faded abruptly. "It's not a gift?"

"It's a loan. The kind you wanted."

She laid her hands on the table. "What's the interest rate?"

"Three percent."

She gasped. "What's the catch?"

"The catch is to pay it back in small weekly installments." He swirled the dark red wine in his glass. "And you have to buy one of our repossessed trucks from the bank. I've never done this before. No one has. From what I've seen of the women I think it'll work. But they'll need your help."

He explained the program to her while she ate her salad. Her eyes never left his as he told her they'd have to fill out application forms, have their needs assessed and attend information meetings before it would be official. Then they'd get their money. Then they could have first pick of the repossessions parked behind the bank before they were auctioned off.

"They'll have checkbooks and deposit slips and everything?" she asked.

He nodded, refilling her glass. It had taken all day. It had taken every ounce of persuasion he had, every bit of clout to persuade the board of directors. It went against every principle they'd agreed on to set things straight in Aruaca. No new agricultural loans. No loans for high-risk creditors, no credit for the self-employed. He'd talked so fast and long that his mouth had hurt.

But he'd convinced them. And himself at the same time. It occurred to him that if it worked they might even extend loans to other self-employed people. If it didn't, he'd feel like a fool, lose his credibility and his ability to do his job here before he'd even looked for the silver mines of Tochabamba.

Her eyes glowed. She reached across the table and took his hand. "Thank you."

He felt the calluses on her palm, the warmth of her skin, and he held her hand for a long moment. Her gaze was warm and steady. She was so sure of herself. Sure of the villagers, sure of their ability. He knew it was just a truck, just one lousy truck, but no one knew where it would take them. No one knew if it would really make a difference. But it had forced him to do something he'd been avoiding for years. To take a chance. He felt as if he were standing on the top of that white-capped mountain out there with the whole world looking up to see if he'd fall flat on his face.

Catherine pulled her hand away and looked around. The piano player had been replaced by a Spanish guitarist playing something lushly romantic that caused shivers up and down her spine. It had to be the music. It couldn't be the touch of his hand on hers. Whatever she felt when he looked at her over his cup of espresso could all be explained. It couldn't be that she was falling for a big-city banker, a man who was more at home in a five-star restaurant than at a hoedown. That would be sheer insanity.

Then how to explain the sparks that flew across the table, the look in his eyes that made it hard to hold her coffee cup with a steady hand? The waiter brought flan in caramel sauce. She took her spoon firmly in hand and let the custard slide down her throat. She sighed contentedly.

"I see why you come here every night," she said. "But you didn't need to bring me along. You could have told me the news in the market."

He shook his head. "This is a business dinner. Besides, I haven't paid you back for the use of your hammock."

"Forget it. Consider it paid back in full. I'll even waive the interest."

He tilted her chin with his thumb. "Maybe you can forget it, but I can't. The interest has been building since the first day I saw you."

She frowned. "Is that why you're doing this? Because you're interested in me?"

"Of course not. This is a chance for me to do something worthwhile. I have to take a risk. If it works, I'll be known as daring and innovative. If it doesn't . . ."

"You'll be known as reckless and foolhardy," she suggested.

"Something like that. And I'll be back in Boston behind my old desk before I know it."

She folded her napkin, and Josh put his credit card on a small silver tray. "Would that be so bad?" she asked.

"To be back in Boston? No. Behind my old desk, yes. It would mean I failed here." The look in his eyes said he wasn't accustomed to failure. "If everything works out, I'll be back in Boston as vice president."

"Vice President Bentley. It has a nice ring to it."

"I've worked hard for it. Besides the loan department, I put in my time in investments and securities. All I needed was some international experience. I could have gone to Panama last year or Colombia the year before, but I was waiting, hoping for Aruaca."

She smiled. "And you got it."

They made their way to the door. The guitar music was louder now and rhythmic. Standing on the sidewalk, Catherine heard city noises far in the background, horns and gears shifting on steep hills. From behind her Josh put his hands on her shoulders.

"There's something else I want to do here," he said.

"You mean you still haven't stemmed the tide of inflation or reduced the national debt?" she asked lightly, trying to ignore the vibrations traveling down her spine.

"Not yet. But I'm working on it."

He ran his hands down her arms, and she shivered involuntarily. The air was cool. His fingers were warm. He pulled her back against his chest, and she felt his heart pounding through his oxford cloth shirt.

Just in the nick of time he caught himself. He almost mentioned the mine. After keeping it a secret all these years, he'd almost blurted it out to a woman he scarcely knew.

"See that?" he said, pointing downtown to a tall building outlined against the ink-blue sky. "That's where I live. On the top floor."

She gasped. A penthouse apartment with a view of the whole city. Before she could speak a taxi pulled up and Josh offered the driver enough money to take them to Palomar.

From the back seat she looked out the window. The moon was hovering over the snows of Teregape. They drove up the street and looked down on a city ablaze with lights. She stifled a yawn. La Luz was a stay-up-late city and she was a go-to-bed-early person. She belonged in the country. She looked at Josh out of the corner of her eye, suave and urbane from his wing-tipped shoes to his dark, close-cropped hair. He belonged in the city. It didn't matter which one. He was at ease eating in a five-star restaurant every night. She wasn't.

Why that made her sad she couldn't say. She'd lived twenty-eight years without ever venturing into such a restaurant and had no need to ever set foot in one again. She was happy with her simple life. Especially now that she was getting the truck. If she weren't so sleepy, she'd be jumping with joy. But her eyelids were drooping. She was determined not to doze through another trip between La Luz and Palomar.

The next thing she knew she was sleeping on Josh's shoulder for the second time that day. She forced her eyes open and looked up at the sky. The stars glowed faintly. She turned to tell him she understood why he couldn't see the constellations in town, but his eyes were closed. His breathing was even and his legs angled off to one side.

She studied his face. Were those worry lines there the last time she looked? Maybe this loan was causing him more concern than he let on. Was he going out on a limb for her and the villagers just to humor her? She wondered what kind of a name he would make for himself if they didn't pay it back. What would happen to his future in the bank if the program failed?

The taxi hit a bump in the road and his briefcase slipped out from under his arm. She set it on the floor, then folded his suit coat and laid it over the front seat. Finally she leaned back and closed her eyes. But at the next steep turn his body swayed across the seat and his head landed on her shoulder. Her eyes flew open. His stayed shut.

She took his shoulders in her hands and firmly edged him back on his side. He groaned. She wedged herself in the corner and resolutely closed her eyes once more. But the next turn sent him careening toward her again.

She sighed. She couldn't wake him and ask him to move when he only had five hours of sleep in the past two days. She couldn't wake him when he felt so right where he was. She liked the way he smelled of American soap. And the way his chin rubbed against her cheek, slightly scratchy and smelling of after-shave, American after-shave.

Familiar, comfortable smells, and yet like nothing she'd ever known before. Like no one she'd ever known before. Was America full of men like this and she just hadn't noticed? Was

Josh Bentley an ordinary man who seemed extraordinary because she'd been buried on the farm? That must be it. Her shaking hands, the banging of her heart, these were the reactions of someone who'd been out of touch.

She told Jacinda she hadn't known any men in America, only boys. And it was true. She had to come all this way to meet a man. Josh Bentley was all man. She was achingly aware of that fact for the next hundred miles as the taxi bounced along the narrow highway.

Josh felt himself sinking into the soft wool of her sweater. It wasn't day and it wasn't night. He wasn't asleep and he wasn't awake. He was somewhere in between, and Catherine was there with him, riding through the darkness. Her hair tumbled over her shoulder and caressed his cheek. He inhaled the fragrance of sunshine and flowers, ordinary homegrown flowers, but like nothing he'd ever smelled before.

He didn't want the ride to end, but the taxi jolted to a stop in front of Catherine's house. He sat up straight and paid the driver. With his briefcase in his hand and his suit jacket over his arm he stood in the road, wishing he could put his arms around her and feel her body melt into his. But she was looking around at her house, at her garden, everywhere but at him.

He felt strange, empty, disoriented. He managed a half smile in the darkness. "Good night. I'll be off just as soon as I fix the car." He opened his briefcase on his knee and took the new hose out.

"I see." She hesitated. He imagined her inviting him in for a cup of coffee or an early breakfast or a nap in the hammock. He could almost smell the coffee, taste the food and feel the hammock sway.

She spoke. "Do you know what to do?"

"Of course. It's just a matter of replacing the hose. They explained it to me at the garage. How hard can it be? I'll be out of here in ten minutes."

She turned toward her house. "Well, thanks for the dinner... and the ride... and the loan."

He watched her go. "You're welcome." It wasn't the way he'd hoped the evening would end, standing there watching her disappear into her house. He stayed for a moment in the warm night air, waiting to see if the gas light he'd seen last night would go on in her bedroom, but the house was dark and quiet.

Maybe she'd taken her nightgown from the hook on the wall and undressed in the kitchen. He pictured the pink sweater coming off over her head. And then her bra.

He looked down, and the ground seemed to rise up to meet him. He was losing it. He had to get out of there. The sooner the better. His car was just where he'd left it. Removing the old hose was easy. He tossed it onto the ground. Fastening the new one in its place was no problem with the screwdriver from the glove compartment. His eyes were getting used to the dark.

He tightened the clamp and cinched it down. One final twist and he'd be heading back down the road to civilization. But the clamp sprang up and snapped in two. He bent over and picked up the useless pieces. Then, very carefully, he closed the hood of the car. He wanted to laugh, he wanted to cry. Most of all he wanted to sleep.

He didn't look back at her house. He didn't think about the hammock. Even if she came out and begged him to come in, he wouldn't go. He had his pride. And he had his car. It didn't run, but he had it. He climbed into the back seat. Out of his jacket he made a pillow. He folded his legs like a jackknife and closed his eyes. What he would do in the morning he didn't know. Right now he didn't care.

When Catherine woke, the sun was streaming through the window, making a rectangular pattern on her bed. She sat up with a guilty start. She'd fallen asleep so fast she hadn't heard Josh's car start up. She imagined him driving through the night, stopping at his apartment and going to the office, while she slept through the raucous rooster's crowing.

After dressing quickly, she walked out through the kitchen to the back of the house. She inhaled deeply the clean air fragrant with sage and rosemary that grew along the fence. It was good to be home. She felt unsettled and anxious in the city. Especially this last time.

There were goats to milk, eggs to collect and melons to pick, but first she had to find Jacinda and tell her the good news.

She walked around the front of her house and stopped dead in her tracks. Josh's car was exactly where he'd left it. She dropped her wicker basket and ran to peer in the back window. He was folded in the back seat, sleeping soundly. She rapped on the window. He raised his head and blinked at her. Her mouth curved into a reluctant smile at the sight of his rumpled, sleepy appearance.

She heard herself asking the obvious question. "What are you doing here?"

He sat up and rubbed his head. She opened the door and stared down at him. "The clamp broke," he said, holding up the two metal pieces.

She took them out of his hand to examine them. "Why didn't you tell me?"

He got out of the car and ran his hand through his hair, feeling like an idiot, his last words still ringing in his ears, and probably in hers, too. "How hard can it be?" And "Out of here in ten minutes." She must be wondering if he was creating these problems as an excuse to hang around.

"What would you have done?" he asked irritably. "Made a new one out of bailing wire?" He paused, regaining control. "Sorry, but it's just a damn inconvenience being so far from . . . from . . ."

"Civilization? Go ahead and say it. We're in the sticks, the boonies. Away from tall buildings and polluted air."

He put his hand on her shoulder. "I'm sorry if I sounded critical. I'm not angry with you. I'm angry with myself. I want to get out of here, and I'm sure you want me out of here as soon as possible so you can go back to your prize potatoes and I can go back to reducing the national debt." He raised the hood of the car. "That's the new hose. But it's no good without the clamp."

She rubbed the broken pieces together thoughtfully in the palm of her hand. "We could try Old Pedro," she said after a moment.

"Old Pedro? Who's Old Pedro? You said all the men were working the tin mines."

"He's too old and crippled. He hurt his leg in a mining accident years ago. Now he makes drain gutters and fixes things."

"What kind of things? Metal things?" he asked. She nodded and he grabbed her arm. "Let's go see him."

With the new hose under his arm and the broken clamp in his pocket, Josh followed Catherine over the same rutted road the taxi had taken last night, past fields of tiny green onion shoots and brilliant tomatoes. He wanted to apologize for being irritable, but the silence had gone on for too long and stretched between them like the road to Old Pedro's shed across the footbridge. He wanted to talk to her about the loan program, but his throat was dry and the walls of his stomach were knocking together.

Yesterday he was on a high. Anything seemed possible. The loan. The truck. Catherine. His career. Today he was racked with doubts. The program was too big, too ambitious. He wanted to absorb some of her confidence. He wanted to run his hands over her cool skin and bury his face in her dark hair. But she had work to do and so did he.

At the end of the path was a small shed with a misshapen figure of a man bent over a piece of corrugated metal with a pair of tin snips. He looked up from his work. A lantern hung from the ceiling and illuminated his lined face. Catherine introduced Old Pedro to Josh, and Pedro peered into his face for a long moment.

Josh brought out the hose and the clamp and Catherine explained what had happened. Old Pedro merely nodded. While they watched he cut and hammered and bent the scrap metal until he had fashioned a rough copy of the broken clamp. Josh breathed a sigh of relief and reached into his wallet, but the old man shook his head with a rush of words in Spanish.

"He says he has done it for a favor," Catherine said. "It is too small a job to accept money."

"But I have nothing else to offer," Josh protested.

"He says not to worry. The gringos have always treated him well. Back in the old days when he worked the mines."

Josh studied the man's wrinkled face and watched him hobble across the dirt floor to see them to the door. "You mean the tin mines," he said.

Catherine translated and Pedro shook his head. *"Plata,"* he said. "Silver."

"Where?" Josh asked.

Old Pedro waved his hand in the general direction of the mountains to the south. "Out there."

"If I wanted to go there, if I wanted to see them, could he show me?"

The eagerness in Josh's voice, the intensity of his gaze, startled her. "I don't think so. He's old as you see, and lame."

"Maybe he could show me on a map. Or tell me how to get there." Josh felt a surge of excitement rush through his veins.

Catherine asked, but the old man shook his head. "He says he couldn't tell you. And he couldn't take you because the God of Thunder closed the entrance and put a curse on the mine before even one piece of silver could be extracted."

Josh stared at the old man. It was just as he had heard. His father and the Tochabamba silver mine. His hopes to strike it rich, to find his fortune. But as usual it slipped away. This time it was an avalanche. It was always something—a natural disaster or unscrupulous partners, but all his life the Tochabamba stood as a symbol of hope and riches and loss.

For a moment Josh felt what his father must have felt on the brink of a discovery, the excitement and the anticipation. And then, just as surely, the disappointment. Outside the entrance in the bright sunshine, Josh hesitated. He had to know, whether he ever got there or not.

"The mine, was it the Tochabamba?"

Without waiting for the translation the old man's eyes widened in surprise. He spoke rapidly in Spanish, gesturing with his short, muscular arms while Josh watched and strained to understand.

"What's he saying?" he demanded.

Catherine's eyebrows drew together. "He says he's surprised you know that name. He's the only one left who remembers around here. The others were killed when the God of Thunder shook the earth."

"Everyone?"

She shook her head. "Everyone but Pedro and the *padrón*. The *padrón* paid off the workers with shares in the mine. Pedro still has his."

"Who was the *padrón?* Where can I find him?"

"He went away for good. Far away. It wasn't safe to stay. It isn't safe to go."

Old Pedro shuffled impatiently, and they thanked him again and left. Josh had one more question, but he already knew the answer. The *padrón* was his father. Escaping death by the skin of his teeth. And coming that close to finding his fortune.

They walked back to the car, the new, improvised clamp in Josh's pocket, thoughts of avalanches and falling rock and silver flooding his mind. Catherine watched silently while he raised the hood, inserted the new hose and tightened the new clamp. He held his breath, but the clamp stayed in place.

He turned to say goodbye, his eyes the clear blue of the sky. But there were lines of fatigue around his mouth, and the shadow of a beard along his jaw. She felt a stab of guilt. She'd slept comfortably in her bed while he was doubled up in the back seat of his car. He'd taken her to dinner. He'd gotten them the loan. She owed him something. She owed him a lot. Besides, she wanted to ask him more about the mine. She touched the sleeve of his wrinkled shirt.

"Come and have breakfast before you go." He looked surprised, and that made her feel guiltier. "It isn't a big deal. Just some coffee and bread. You must be hungry."

"I am," he said, and they walked into the house where it was dark and cool. While she watched he ate four slices of bread spread thickly with sweet butter and strawberry jam. She refilled his coffee cup and sat down across from him at the rough-hewn pine table.

"How did you know about the Tochabamba Mine?" she asked.

"From my father."

She set her coffee on the table. "Was he the *padrón?*"

"Yes. I don't know why, but I'm sure he was. So I'm not the only one holding shares to a worthless silver mine."

"You said your father had incredible stories to tell." A vision of a small boy, his blue eyes round with wonder, filled her mind.

He nodded. "That was one of them. The one I liked best." He rubbed his hand across his chin. "It had everything—danger, treasure and excitement. It was such a good story that when I grew up I wondered if it was true." His gaze drifted over her shoulder to the window, to the fields, to the faint outline of the mountains beyond. There was a longing there she couldn't ignore. She put her hand on his.

"I'll talk to him again. I'll ask him where the mine was. We'll get a map and go look for it," she said impulsively, catching the excitement, sensing that there was more than silver at stake.

His gaze turned from the horizon back to the room. Back to reality. "No, don't bother him. It's not important. There's probably nothing there."

Puzzled by his sudden change of mood, she shrugged. "Whatever you want."

Abruptly he stood and pulled her up from the chair with him, his hands holding hers tightly. "This is what I want," he said. Her heart pounded so loudly that he heard it. He'd shared his secret with her, and now he wanted to share even more. How much more he wasn't sure.

He kissed her forehead, and she lifted her face to his. The look in her eyes told him she wanted this as much as he did, that she'd been waiting for this moment for days, for weeks, forever. A voice in his head told him he couldn't afford this kind of distraction, that already he'd let her influence him too much. More than she should.

He could still stop. It wasn't too late, the voice in his head told him. But whatever the voice said, his brain chose not to hear. Instead his lips chose to brush against hers, testing her response. Just one kiss, he thought, one kiss after all this time. But when she buried her fingers in his hair his control snapped. He covered her mouth with his and kissed her over and over with all the force of his pent-up desire.

Her arms tightened around his neck. Her kisses were sweeter than the jam she had made, warmer than the freshly baked bread. And he couldn't get enough. The more she gave the more he wanted. Finally they pulled apart, breathless and panting. His heart banged against his ribs. It was excitement; it was panic. He had to get out of there while he still knew what he was doing. Before he picked her up and headed for a hayloft somewhere. Before they did something they'd both regret.

He jerked himself back to the present. Unsteadily he walked to the open door. She followed him. "Thanks for the breakfast." His voice was like gravel. He paused and ran his hand lightly over her dark hair. He was sorry. Not sorry he'd kissed her, but sorry he didn't have room in his life for a woman like this. His goals lay ahead of him almost within reach: his promotion and security. He couldn't afford any distractions. No women, no silver mines.

Breathless and shaken, she followed him to the car, wondering what it all meant. She stood there, making a dent in the dirt with the heel of her shoe while he started the engine. She leaned down and looked through the window. "When will I see you again?" she asked.

"Friday," he answered. "Can you bring your group to the bank in the morning?"

"Yes, sure." She clenched her hands tightly at her sides. Her stomach churned. She told herself it meant nothing to him. It was just a kiss or two, that was all. She forced herself to think about the loan. It was really going to happen. He'd made it happen. She was grateful for that. He reached for her, holding her face in his hands, mesmerizing her with his eyes. Then he kissed her again, slowly and thoroughly. Trembling, she pulled away. Without a word he drove off into the dust.

She watched until his car was out of sight. Long after it was gone she stayed rooted to the ground, staring straight ahead to the horizon. Thinking about the distance between them, she felt an overwhelming sense of loss. But there was more than the miles separating them. Much more. He was obviously a man with a dream. What business was it of hers if he refused to follow it?

She had other things to worry about. At the sound of a bleating goat she turned and faced the chores she had to do every day. She couldn't let thoughts of Josh and his father's mine interfere with her own life. She coaxed the goat into the yard and brought a clean bucket from the shed. She tried to think about making goat cheese and how to sell it, but in her mind she traveled across mountains to a distant mine, where a man could find his dream and a woman could make it come true.

Chapter Five

A more unlikely group never stood at the entrance to the International Bank of La Luz, Catherine thought. They chattered nervously. They tapped their feet on the marble steps. They giggled at the sight of secretaries in tight skirts and high heels. They were only a few miles from the Rodriguez Market, but the street where the bank was located was in another world of trees and flowers and monuments. On Friday morning it was filled with traffic and people on their way to work.

With one last word of encouragement to the women Catherine pushed the heavy glass door open and stepped inside. The women fell silent. Suddenly she regretted her decision to wear her peasant clothes. She felt as out of place as they must feel in this high-ceilinged lobby with its marble floor. She wiped her palms on her skirt and told a man behind a desk that she wanted to see Mr. Bentley. He gave her a doubtful look but picked up the phone.

By the time Josh reached the lobby, Catherine had convinced herself she'd dreamed the whole thing. The kiss, the loan and the truck. But when she saw him their eyes locked and held. And the unspoken message calmed her nerves and soothed her psyche. Yes, I remember, he telegraphed across the room, and she felt the heat rise to her face.

She smiled at Josh. He smiled at the women. It was a beautiful day. It was a historic day. They went to a room where they heard a man explain the loan process, slowly and clearly with pictures, in Spanish and in Mamara. The women leaned forward, hanging on every word.

Catherine's eyes glazed over with joy. They were beginning a new era. She stood at the back of the room, too choked up to speak.

Josh pressed his shoulder against hers. "Do you think it will work?"

"It has to," she said under her breath.

After the session, the women went back to the market and Catherine stayed behind to look at the repossessed trucks parked behind the bank in a parking lot. She gave Josh her hat to hold while she raced the engines, pounded the tires and tested the brakes.

"I don't know," she said, looking down at him from the driver's seat. "I hate to think of our profiting from someone else's loss."

He opened the door and held out his hand to help her down. "The somebody elses were drug dealers, if that makes you feel any better. The government confiscated their houses, their cars and their jewels. We got their trucks before they even got a chance to use them."

"Oh, well, in that case." She didn't allow herself to think of where this truck might end up if they had to default on their loan.

"This one?" he asked.

"This one," she said firmly. "I can't wait for them to see it. I can't wait to drive it."

They walked back to the bank. "You're not afraid?"

"Afraid? I've been driving tractors bigger than this since I was fourteen years old."

He held the door open for her. He liked the way her chin tilted up. He admired the way her eyes sparkled when she was excited and he enjoyed the pleasure the truck brought her. If the whole thing failed and he wound up behind a loan officer's desk in Boston, he'd remember her eyes, warm and soft or dancing with delight. But in the meantime ... They stood on the wide front steps.

The sun was directly overhead. A shoeshine boy appeared from nowhere and approached Josh. He shook his head absently and looked at his watch. "What about lunch?"

She shook her head. "I've already missed a half day of work. I'm terrible at bargaining, but I'm useful in other ways."

A smile stole over his face. "I'm sure you are."

She looked down at her dusty shoes, then back to meet his gaze. "When can we have the truck? Today?"

"If I stay late and work on the papers. Do you have a license to drive it here?"

"I got one when I arrived, just in case. I'll send the women home with Tomás. Next week they'll apply for their permits. When should I come back?"

He set her hat firmly on her head and let his fingers trail across her smooth cheek to her chin. "Soon."

She nodded and then she was gone, down the steps on rope-soled shoes before he could give her money for a taxi. He started after her, but she disappeared into the lunchtime crowd. The sun shone just as brightly after she was gone, and the air was just as warm. But there was something missing. Catherine.

She was interfering with his work. She was disturbing his sleep. He wanted her around all the time, but that wasn't possible. The next thing he knew she'd talk him into going to the mine or borrowing more money for something else.

She came at five o'clock. He was pacing back and forth when she walked through the door. He told her the license was ready, but the ownership papers weren't processed yet. They could check back later. What he didn't tell her was that even when the papers were ready he wasn't going to let her drive home alone in the dark, no matter how much experience she'd had with trucks and tractors.

She nodded and he looked around. Customers were still waiting for tellers. Bank officials were in deep discussions with important clients behind closed doors. Banks and stores stayed open until 7:00. Josh usually worked late. But not tonight. Not with Catherine standing there with one braid over her shoulder, her face tilted up to his, her expression hopeful and expectant. He had a wild desire to grab her arm, run out the front door and get lost in the bustling, vibrant city out there.

He did the next best thing. He led her firmly out the door with his hand on her elbow.

"Where are we going?" she asked.

"I don't know. You know the city better than I do. Take me somewhere I haven't been before. That won't be hard. I haven't been anywhere."

"Anywhere?" Her eyes sparkled and her lips curved in an enticing smile.

A rush of dizziness engulfed him, and he steadied himself by holding her arms. After weeks of living and working within a four-block radius, he had a desire to expand his horizon. "Anywhere," he said.

They started down the avenue, past galleries filled with silver, pewter and antiques. They mingled with shoppers, workers and Indians dressed like Catherine and bureaucrats dressed like Josh. The sun was setting on the flatlands that surrounded the city, and a cool wind threatened to send Catherine's hat flying. In front of the San Francisco Church at the end of the street, he stopped to take it off her head and smooth her hair. He longed to loosen the braid, to feel the masses of dark hair in his hands.

The stone-carved statue of Saint Francis in front of the church smiled benevolently, but they didn't linger. Catherine took his hand and led him around the corner down an alley lined with small, elegant shops. In front of a store crammed with soft leather goods she paused.

"Have you ever been to a *peña?*" she asked.

He turned her hat on the palm of his hand. "I don't think so. What is it?"

"An open-air restaurant with typical food and folk music. You've been in La Luz for a month and nobody's taken you to a *peña?*" she asked increduously.

"Nobody's taken me anywhere . . . except to the Rodriguez Market. They told me I could find everything I needed there.

They were right." He gave her a smile that made her heart skip a beat. She folded her arms across her waist. Deliberately she tilted her head and surveyed his suit jacket. Her gaze lingered on his vest.

"What's wrong?" he asked.

"It gets cold at the *peña* after the sun sets. You need a sweater."

He opened the door for her to the brightly lighted shop, and they breathed deeply of the warm, earthy smell of leather. "What about a jacket?"

"You'd buy a leather jacket just like that?"

"I need a leather jacket. I've always needed one. I just didn't know it until now."

Hearing this, an attentive clerk slipped up behind him and helped him remove his suit coat. His vest came off next. The first jacket he tried on was brown with wide shoulders and tucked in around the waist. It made him look like a World War II flying ace.

Catherine couldn't stop staring. Where was the conservative banker, the one who ate at the same restaurant every night? She warned herself he was still there, just a breath away, under a layer of leather. But here was a man who was buying himself a jacket so he could go to a new restaurant. Here was a man who was taking a chance on a group of poor women on the strength of his intuition and her recommendation.

In a momentary panic she wondered what she'd started the day she had barged her way into his office. But it had begun before that. On the day he had walked up to her with mangoes in his hand and refused to bargain.

He was watching her face. "What's wrong? Is it too casual?"

She shook her head. She couldn't trust her voice. It was the warmth of the shop, the rich smell of leather, not the overwhelming desire to touch the jacket, to slide her hands inside and run her palms over the soft cotton of his button-down shirt across the flat planes of his chest, she told herself. He was waiting for her to answer.

"No, it's fine, but..." She pulled him aside. "You can't bargain here. The prices are fixed," she whispered.

"I know," he whispered back, his lips brushing her ear. While the clerk wrapped up his suit coat and vest he noticed a rack of leather belts, and examined the workmanship. "Do you think Old Pedro would like one of these?" he asked Catherine.

She ran her fingers over the thick cowhide and looked up inquiringly.

"I saw he carried his tools in his pockets," Josh said. "There's a pouch for his tape measure and loops for his tin snips."

Touched by his thoughtfulness, she nodded. "Yes, I think he'd like it."

He told the clerk to add the belt to his bill. After he paid, they left the shop and headed toward the Peña Murilla.

"Is it just a thank-you present?" Catherine asked, her hair loosened by the wind, curling in tendrils around her face. "Or were you thinking of asking him again to take you to the mine?"

He took her arm unconsciously and gripped it tightly. "I know there's nothing there. But maybe I should try to go, anyway. Does that make sense?"

She nodded and her heart lifted. She didn't say anything, but maybe the man was coming to grips with his heritage, after all.

Heads turned as they walked, for a second look at the tall man in the brown leather jacket and the beautiful hatless Mamara Indian woman at his side who walked with such easy confidence. Her braid was tossed to one side, her skirts were blown to show her ankles, and the wind had whipped color into her cheeks.

At the end of the street they opened a gate to the Peña Murillo. Under an arbor they sat next to each other at a long table lined with people where the food was served family style. Catherine passed platter after platter of stuffed pastries to the end of the table. She noticed that Josh ate everything that came his way. So far the *peña* was a success.

He set his fork down. "Did you notice that the people across from us are staring, wondering why someone who looks like you is with someone who looks like me?"

"You're imagining things. People are here to eat and listen to the music. Besides you look fine."

He grinned. "You look fine, too. Very fine."

His blue eyes met her dark, long-lashed eyes, and from somewhere far away the faint sound of a wooden Indian flute came floating through the air. She wanted to turn to watch the musicians approach, but she was trapped in a trance, bound by Josh on one side and the haunting melody on the other.

She had heard this music before, but never had it touched her so deeply with its melancholy sweetness. When the flutist stopped, the spell was broken. Josh put his hand on the back of her neck and drew her close to him.

"I've never heard anything like it," he whispered.

His breath was warm on her lips. The lights were dim. "There's more," she promised.

There was a many-stringed cousin to the guitar that sounded more mellow and softer than anything she'd ever heard, and after that a carved-out gourd sent out primitive vibrations through the air, filling her with a sweet sadness. Her fingers gripped Josh's tightly, and from the pressure she knew he felt as she did.

When it was over, they sat without clapping, still holding hands. In a daze they moved to the exit and stood on the street again, gazing at the moon casting its silver glow on snow-capped Teregape. It took a few minutes for Catherine to return to reality.

Josh spoke first. "You told me it was a restaurant. You didn't tell me it was an out-of-body experience."

"It isn't. I mean, it never was before. Everything was different tonight." She looked around the empty alley. "We've got to go. I have to get home. Can I get my truck now?"

"No."

"No? You said we'd check back later. You said your secretary was working on it."

"She was, but she isn't anymore. She's gone home. It's too late for you to drive home alone on that road."

The blood rushed to her head. "I told you I've driven trucks like that since..."

"Since you were fourteen years old. I know. But not to-night. Tonight I'm driving you home."

She glared at him. "I suppose I ought to thank you. But I don't feel much like it."

He took her firmly by the elbow. "I understand. Naturally you're disappointed."

"You could say that."

They walked briskly in the direction of the bank. "You've gotten along for eighteen months without a truck. You can wait until tomorrow."

"We don't come to town until Thursday."

"Okay, Thursday."

"I should have waited for the transfer papers. I should never have left the bank without our truck. Is it our truck, or not?"

"Not. The bank holds the papers until the loan is paid off." He looked at his watch. "That'll be in about ten years. Until then I have to protect the bank's interests. I don't want the truck going off the road in the middle of the night before you've even made the first payment."

They stopped abruptly in front of the bank, and she waited while he went to get his car from the parking lot. She paced back and forth, seething in anger. Her fingers itched to hold the steering wheel of the truck. She'd planned to drive up in front of Jacinda's house in the morning and watch the children come running from all over the neighborhood. He didn't trust her to get the truck back in the dark. He didn't believe she was capable enough. But she was. She'd show him.

Josh drove out of the lot and around the front of the bank to pick her up. He could see by the set of her shoulders how angry she was, but he didn't care. It was better to endure her resentment than to lie awake all night wondering if she'd made it back to Palomar. He reached across to fasten her seat belt. His arm grazed the tips of her breasts. He heard the sharp in-take of her breath. Suddenly he thought of the music and the vibrations from the instruments humming in the night air and the feeling of her hand in his, and he wished he hadn't spoiled the mood. But he'd had no choice. He could tell by her icy si-lence that he'd convinced her that his first concern was the truck. Now if only he could convince himself of that.

Where had he gone wrong? When had this ceased to be a business transaction and become a personal matter? Was it the first day at the farm riding behind her on the horse with the warm sun shining on her hair? No, it was before that. It was that day in the market when he stood in front of her and paid too much for the mangoes. Since the first moment he'd seen her she'd had that effect on him. Of undermining his better judgment.

If it weren't for her, he wouldn't have made this risky loan. His dream of finding the silver mine would have remained a dream. His private dream. There was something about her that caused him to do things he had no business doing. What was it? Her earthy sensuality? Her idealism? Her relentless optimism?

He glanced sideways at her profile. The purity of the outline of her cheek touched him somewhere deep within himself and resolutely he turned his attention back to the road ahead. From now on he would keep his dreams to himself, his loans to a minimum and his mind on his work.

An evening like this, of music and vibrations and the nearness of Catherine, was enough to pull him off course, to distract him from his goals. He was here to do a job, to help this country and to help himself rise to the top of his profession. He wouldn't be led astray as his father was by romantic dreams of riches buried in the ground. There were riches to be had, yes, but they came from years of hard work.

Catherine didn't sleep on the way home. It hurt to realize how little confidence Josh had in her, both in her ability to drive and her ability to pay back the loan. Well, she'd show him. They'd work so hard they'd pay off the loan in five years. Of course, she wouldn't be around in five years, but she'd be sure they were well on their way by the time she left. If it was the last thing she did. It just might be.

When they reached her little house, she gave him a curt goodbye and a reminder they'd be in Thursday for the truck. Catherine felt guilty for treating him rudely, but her pride wouldn't let her relent.

The next day she told the women about the truck. They were excited, but not as excited as they were about Doña Blanca's daughter's engagement to Jacinda's youngest son. The young man had come home from the mines over the weekend with a month's salary in one hand and a ring in the other. Jacinda was pleased with the dowry and quickly gave her blessing, perhaps partly because the bride was already three months pregnant.

"Yes," she said to Catherine as she lingered in the doorway to Catherine's kitchen the next morning, "I am well pleased. Not as pleased as I will be when we celebrate your wedding, but pleased all the same."

Catherine looked up over the pot of boiling water she was sterilizing jam jars in and gave Jacinda a stern look. "I know you consider me an old maid, and I suppose you're not the only one. But there are other things to do in this day and age besides getting married. For myself I've chosen to use my knowledge to help people like yourself improve their farming methods. After I leave Palomar at the end of the two years, I'll go on to another country, another valley, another farm. Surely you can see there's no room for a man in my life."

"What about Señor Bentley?" the older woman asked.

"What about him? Are you suggesting he accompany me on my travels? He's our banker, that's all," she said so emphatically that Jacinda took a step backward. "I'm only interested in the money he's loaning us, and he's only interested in making sure we make our payments."

Jacinda bobbed her head. "I know. I know. Did I not hear all about it in the bank yesterday? Payments and interest and credit and notes until my head was spinning."

Catherine frowned. "I hope you paid attention. Because if we miss one payment, the truck goes back to the bank. We don't really own it until we make all of our payments."

"With the little stubs from the little book. I remember," Jacinda assured her.

Catherine nodded. She had been paying attention. They all had. She felt a pang of guilt for treating Jacinda like a child. For talking down to her just as Josh had done to her. And for talking business when Jacinda wanted to talk weddings. But she had a splitting headache. Farm girls who stayed up late paid a price the next day, but she had no right to take out her anger toward Josh on Jacinda.

She poured two cups of tea from the kettle on the stove and motioned for her old friend to sit down. "Where will they live?" she asked.

Jacinda spooned a dollop of honey into her tea. "Since Juan Carlos works in the mines, Magdalena will continue to live at home until the baby comes. Then they will have to find a home of their own." She sipped her tea. "We have much to do in two weeks."

"Two weeks?" Catherine set her cup down with a thud.

Jacinda nodded. "Clothes to be made. Food to be cooked. You have never seen a village wedding with a piñata and a whole roasted lamb and dancing. Mr. Bentley has never seen such a wedding, either, I suppose."

"Mr. Bentley? I don't think Mr. Bentley is interested in weddings," she said, rubbing her forehead with the back of her hand.

Jacinda took Catherine's cup and stared into the leaves at the bottom. "Perhaps not," she murmured, "but I know Doña Blanca will invite him all the same. Sometimes men surprise you."

Catherine had to agree with that. Just when you thought men were sweet, sensitive and kind, they turned out to be devious and self-centered.

Jacinda tilted the teacup and grasped Catherine's arm. "This is truly amazing," she said breathlessly. "Just as we speak of marriage I see something about it in your tea leaves."

"Really?" Catherine suppressed a smile. "What is it?"

"A village wedding. But the bride is not Magdalena. The bride is you. In a flowing white gown with a veil. You are smiling and saying, 'Thank you, Jacinda.'"

"And who might the groom be?" Catherine asked innocently.

Jacinda shrugged. "I cannot see his face, but he is very rich. He showers you with silver coins."

"Silver? How delightful," Catherine enthused. Then deliberately she reached across the table for Jacinda's cup and studied the leaves at the bottom. "What have we here? What I see in your future is a big white truck with you riding next to me in front with all your friends from the market looking on enviously. It will happen soon. Very soon."

Jacinda met Catherine's eyes and said no more about Catherine's wedding. Catherine told her that on Thursday they would surely leave town in their truck. Or rather the bank's truck. She and the women would all go in together to pick it up. She knew Josh would have to come through. He couldn't take twenty women home in his car. And he couldn't invite twenty women to dinner at Restaurante Roberto.

He couldn't distract twenty women by wearing a leather jacket, either, or showering them with attention. It would be all business. That was the way he wanted it and that was the way it would be. Sign the transfer of sale, get in the truck and come home.

But on Thursday, as they waited in the cool, high-ceilinged lobby of the bank, she didn't feel quite so calm. She wiped her palms on her shawl and tried not to look anxious. She saw him before he saw her, but not by much. Just enough time to notice he was wearing a gray suit with pinstripes that fit his lanky body without a wrinkle. Just enough to take a deep breath, but not enough time to stop her knees from shaking under her layered skirts.

Josh knew she'd been angry when she got out of his car and coolly wished him a safe trip back to town, but he didn't expect it to last, and he didn't expect to be hurt by her cool, distant air as they put their signatures to the loan agreement and the transfer of sale. He was sure now she had no interest in him except for the loan. Since that was what he wanted, he didn't know why it bothered him, but it did. He tried to take her aside to talk to her, but the women were always there, separating him from her as if she'd arranged it that way. They thanked him and shook his hand, all of them, except Catherine.

Before he had a chance to speak to her they were in the parking lot, piling into the long bed of the truck with their empty burlap sacks, Jacinda and Doña Blanca next to Catherine in the cab. He told her to drive carefully. He wanted to warn her about taking the curves too fast, but he remembered her telling him not to treat her like a child, and he bit his tongue.

He stood in the lot and watched them drive away, the women squealing with delight. In the rearview mirror he caught her eye, and just for a split second she flashed a triumphant smile that said it all. They had their truck and nothing could stop them now.

He thought of her driving on those mountain roads in the dusk and he broke out in a cold sweat. It was one thing to try out the truck in the parking lot, but the thought of her on the rough two-lane road scared the hell out of him.

The next three days were more hell. He had no way of knowing if they'd arrived home or if they'd make it back to town. On Monday morning at dawn he was standing on a rough cobblestone street keeping company with stray dogs and city police in green uniforms who were clearing the road for the trucks arriving from the valleys below.

Finally they came, swaying from side to side like all the other trucks, laden with crates. He felt a knot of tension dissolve in his chest. Of course they weren't like all the other peasants. They were in their own truck with their own driver. Leaning over the edge of the wooden slats that held the produce in place, they called to him.

"Señor Bentley. Look, look at us," they yelled in Spanish.

A smile spread cross his face. He waved to them and they waved back. He watched them unload. They patted the sides of the truck proudly with the palms of their hands when they passed. He picked up a sack of lettuce and fell into step beside Catherine.

"Any problems?" he asked in a carefully casual voice.

"No." She quickened her pace, but if she thought she'd lose him, she was wrong. "Your truck is in perfect shape, so you can stop worrying."

"I'm not worried about the truck. I'm worried about you." The words came out in spite of himself.

She slanted him a cool glance. "Well, you can stop worrying about me. I'm an excellent driver."

"I'm sure you are." He lowered the sack of lettuce behind the stall. She set her sack next to his and put her hands on her hips. Jacinda stepped between Catherine and Josh and began unpacking her peppers as if she was unaware of any tension in the air.

"Señor Bentley," she said with a wide smile, "my son is getting married on the last day of the month. Doña Blanca has asked me to invite you to the wedding, since it is her daughter who is marrying my son."

Josh looked puzzled. He caught a few words, but missed most of it. Jacinda tugged at Catherine's sleeve. "Tell him what I said."

Catherine repeated the message, then added her own words. "Don't feel obligated to come. I told her you're a very busy person."

Josh looked over her head at Jacinda. "I would like to come," he said slowly in Spanish. "Very much."

Jacinda nudged Catherine in the ribs, then danced away to tell the others. Without Jacinda as a buffer they stood looking at each other in awkward silence. Finally Catherine spoke. "The women are so excited about the wedding. They have a lot of sewing and baking to do. On the other hand, the tomatoes are ripe."

"Can I help?" he offered.

"Pick tomatoes? I doubt it."

"When they come into the bank tonight to make their deposit, I'll give them a pep talk. There's a lot riding on their success. If it works..."

"You'll get your promotion."

A muscle twitched in his jaw. The implication of self-interest was unmistakable and hurt him as if she'd stabbed him with a knife. He took her by the shoulders and held her while the women around them froze, watching the scene with wide-eyed fascination.

"Don't put words in my mouth," he said, his voice tight with anger. "I made this loan against my better judgment. But I want it to succeed as much for your sakes as for mine. If it does, they can go on to make a business out of farming, not just subsistence. If they have a business, the men might be able to come home from the mines and work the land with them.

Who knows? Maybe they could dam up the river and make a mill." His blue eyes blazed.

There was complete silence in the stall when he finished talking. Everyone had their eyes on Josh, straining to understand why he was so angry with their beautiful, good-natured Catherine. Only Catherine knew, and her cheeks burned. But he wasn't finished yet.

"I don't know what kind of bankers you've dealt with in the past, but I think I should be judged on my own merits or faults. I gave you the loan because I believed in you, whether I was right or wrong. It may not be the smartest thing I ever did, but I did it and I'm going to do everything I can to make it work out for you.

"But it isn't going to work if you're going to resist every time I try to help you. Yes, I want you to be successful and pay it off. Sure that will make me look good. But it will make the villagers look even better, and then they can go on to bigger things. But to make it work we need each other, you, me and them." He let her go, but she could feel the pressure of his fingers on her skin after he went up the street, out of the market and back to the bank.

Without speaking she unloaded a crate of melons with trembling fingers. The other women followed her example, and soon they were laughing, arguing and bargaining as they did every day. Jacinda's eyes were full of questions, but she confined her conversation with Catherine to the number of sheep in the dowry and the color of her dress.

Catherine answered calmly, but underneath she was a torrent of emotions. She was ashamed of herself. She knew that deep down Josh wasn't only interested in his career. He'd pretended to be, but he wasn't. He'd even made plans for the farm. Far beyond what she'd ever dreamed of. She wished she didn't have to see him at the end of the day. She knew she ought to apologize, but she dreaded it.

At dusk they counted their money. They packed their goods in the truck and spread burlap over the crates. The women were excited. It had been a good day. For making money, but not for making friends, Catherine thought. They walked to the bank, the cash tied in cloth sacks deep in their pockets. Josh was waiting for them. She let the women go first. They spread out the money on the counter and counted it in front of him.

They were doing it all without her, and they were proud of themselves. They should be. For the first time there was no driver to pay off at the end of the day. The women were going to a conference room with a big blackboard and a man who spoke Mamara. They each had a deposit slip in hand. It was their second lesson, and this time it was for real. They had real money and they would make a real deposit. Catherine turned to share the moment with Josh, but he wasn't there.

Maybe he was called away to speak to another client. She thought of going to the receptionist and asking to speak to him, but she didn't. She wasn't ready. But she was ready on the next trip. She'd had time to memorize her speech.

"You were right," she'd say. "There was no reason to drive home in the middle of the night. I was so excited about the truck I wasn't thinking clearly. Thank you for taking me to dinner and thank you for wanting to help us."

Then they would shake hands and it would clear the air. Then the potatoes would start growing again and the berries would ripen on schedule and everything would be right with the world. But he wasn't there. The other man who was handling their account was there and spoke to them. Catherine looked around the lobby from the telephone to the receptionist, but she left without asking for Josh.

When he didn't appear on the next two market days, Jacinda took time out from wedding talk to broach the subject with Catherine on the way home.

"I have not seen Señor Bentley lately," she said casually. "Not since the day you and he exchanged sharp words in the stall."

"Really?" Catherine's tone was light, but her knuckles were white as her fingers tightened on the steering wheel.

"Yes, really," Jacinda answered firmly. "Have you?"

Catherine wrinkled her nose thoughtfully. "I don't think so."

Jacinda watched her negotiate a steep turn. "You know what we say in Spanish."

Catherine braced herself for a barrage of wise sayings that Jacinda kept on hand for every occasion. "What's that?"

"A woman without a man is like a garden without a fence."

Catherine shifted as she headed down a steep grade. "Who needs a fence? Not me. If ever I find a man, it will be one who doesn't fence me in. And what about you? You're not fenced in."

Jacinda clicked her tongue. "We are discussing your life, not mine. Mine is nearly over. Yours is just beginning. Now I heard that in your country you do not use a matchmaker. You marry for love, and yet so many divorces! My girls are all well married, and now my last son is about to become a husband and a father, all thanks to my help. And I will not rest until I have done the same for you."

Catherine sighed. "Jacinda, I appreciate what you want to do, but—"

The old woman put her hand on Catherine's arm. "Do not thank me until your engagement is announced."

"But I told you—"

"That he was not interested in weddings, but you were wrong. He is coming to the wedding. That is a good sign."

"I think I told you I was only interested in the money he could lend us," Catherine said gently.

Jacinda yawned and leaned her head back. "I know. But love is the fruit of marriage. That you are interested in something about him is another good sign. A good beginning." She closed her eyes to indicate that the conversation was over, and the smile that lingered on her lips showed her satisfaction in having the last word.

Chapter Six

The week before the wedding skies were cloudy, while excitement rose to a crescendo. Catherine was relieved to see that the women didn't ignore the harvest. They picked tomatoes all day and sewed a quilt for Magdalena in the evenings around the table in Catherine's kitchen. Profits increased. Every time they went to the bank they watched the numbers in the bank book rise. Josh would have been proud of them if he had been there, but he wasn't. Señor Duran, their loan officer, said he was on a business trip.

Catherine didn't ask when he'd be back. She knew Jacinda would be disappointed if he didn't come to the wedding. But it wasn't her business. It wasn't her wedding. Still, she thought about it all week.

Early in the morning on the day of the wedding she stood on the front steps of the small frame village church and looked up at the darkening sky. The church was small, but large enough to hold all the guests and keep them dry if it rained. It was the outdoor reception she was worried about.

The wind lifted the hem of her filmy summer dress, and she held tightly on to the wide brim of her straw hat with the lavender ribbon. The air was heavy with moisture. They needed rain. They prayed for rain, but not until after the wedding.

Inside the church she walked up to the altar to arrange bunches of flowers that she'd picked before dawn that morning. She buried her face in a bouquet of roses still wet with dew and inhaled their fragrance. From the rear of the church the door creaked and a gust of air blew up the aisle. She whirled around. Holding a yellow rose in one hand, she looked up expectantly.

It took Josh's eyes a few seconds to focus in the dim light. They hadn't told him what time to come. He was looking for the bride. He found Catherine. The door slammed shut behind him, and he breathed the air inside, warm and heavy with the scent of roses.

"You're early," she said, her voice trembling so slightly he almost didn't notice.

He leaned against the door and crossed his arms over his chest. "I didn't know what time it started. I've been out of town and out of touch."

She lifted a vase onto the altar and began filling it with lilies. "I heard you were away on business."

He walked partway up the aisle. "Yes. Duran tells me everything went so smoothly you didn't even miss me." There was a long silence. Behind the tall stalks of lilies she paused and looked at him. He couldn't stand the suspense. He had to know. "Did you?"

She came out from behind the flowers and stepped down, her hat framing her face like a Botticelli painting. "Yes, I missed you. I wanted to tell you—" she stopped and took a breath of air "—that I'm sorry I implied you were an opportunist. I'm really grateful for all you've done for us."

He shook his head. "It's my fault. I told you if I succeeded here I'd come out with a promotion. What else could you think?"

She ran her finger around the petals of the flower in her hand. "You also told me you went out on a limb for us. If we fail, it will make you look bad."

"It looks as if you're not going to fail. Duran tells me your receipts are high. You're keeping up with your payments. If this continues, it would be possible to make other loans to the rest of the market, farmers and artisans, too."

"Really?" She walked forward until they were only inches apart. He nodded. The scent of flowers was everywhere. In her hair, on her skin and in the air. He'd never seen her in a dress. A dress with tiny buttons up the front he couldn't keep his eyes off.

A side door opened and the priest from the next village appeared in a brown robe tied with a cord at the waist. He began lighting candles, and the glow filled the church. Catherine looked at her watch. "You'd better go," she said softly. "I have to finish my work." She broke off the stem of a red rose and leaned forward to put it in his buttonhole. He caught her fingers with his hand. There was a tiny pinprick, a spot of blood on her finger. His touch was so gentle, her eyes misted over.

"What is it?" he asked. "Did you hurt yourself?"

She shook her head and gave him a watery smile. "I always cry at weddings."

"It hasn't even started," he noted.

She bit her lip. "I know." She turned abruptly and went back to the flowers.

He stared at her for a long moment, taking in the curve of her hips in the pale dress, the cloud of her dark hair spilling over her shoulders. Then he left and went to stand in front of the church.

Soon they came, by twos and threes, on horseback, in carts and on foot. All the women he knew and the men he didn't know, stiff and formal in their Sunday best. Even Old Pedro, arriving on his burro, was wearing a suit jacket over a white shirt, the cuffs covering his gnarled hands. He nodded to Josh but didn't approach.

The women greeted Josh with cries of delight and proudly introduced him to their husbands, home from the mine for the occasion. They spoke slowly so he could understand how happy they were to see him, and a warm feeling filled his heart, a strange feeling of belonging.

Josh hardly recognized Jacinda as she alighted from her horse-drawn cart with ribbons twined around the reins and flowers twisted over the horse's ears. Splendid in her long dress, with silver hoops dangling from her ears, she beamed at Josh and presented her son, the bridegroom.

When the church doors opened, Josh followed the crowd and took a seat at the back, saving a place for Catherine. She slid in next to him just as the music began and put her hand in his. His heart thudded against his chest.

"A last-minute problem with the veil," she whispered. "The flower girl stepped on it and I had to sew it up."

Now the guests were on their feet, craning their necks for a glimpse of the bride. First came the flower girls in short white dresses with rings of daisies on their heads. Then the ring bearer, Magdalena's little cousin. And finally Magdalena, her veil firmly in place, her eyes on the bouquet of sunflowers in her hands.

"A symbol of fertility," Catherine whispered.

Jacinda's son stood waiting at the altar, wearing a starched white shirt and a solemn expression. When the bride approached, a look of awe stole over his face, and Catherine gave Josh a sideways glance. He turned her hand over in his and held it tightly.

The ceremony lasted a long time, but Josh didn't mind. There was something about the ebb and flow of the words in Spanish, the feeling of Catherine's hand in his, the glow of candles and the scent of roses that made him want it to go on forever.

But finally the young couple turned and came down the aisle, and the bells rang out from the steeple across the countryside. The guests stood in front of the church armed with handfuls of tiny grains of wheat to throw. Josh examined the wheat in the palm of his hand.

"Another fertility symbol?" he asked.

She nodded. "Flowers, seeds, shells, horns. All the decorations are symbols of strength or fertility. Not that they need them," she said under her breath. "Magdalena is... uh...expecting. It's not a shotgun wedding," she assured him. "It's just with the men away it's hard to find a time to get married. They've been engaged forever. Jacinda and Doña Blanca arranged it long ago, at birth probably. Jacinda's a great believer in arranged marriages." She sighed. "If only she'd forget about arranging mine."

"It must be a real challenge finding someone good enough for you."

"She was about to give up when you came along in your three-piece suit."

"Me?"

"We're the only North Americans she knows, so naturally she thinks it would be a great match."

"And you don't?"

"I don't think it's enough that we come from the same country. I think two people ought to have something more in common." She looked up at him from under the brim of her hat, and suddenly the sun came out. Before he could answer the crowd oohed and ahhed. "It's a good sign," she explained, looking up at the sky. "Happy is the bride the sun shines on."

Just before the couple pulled away Magdalena leaned across her new husband and threw her bouquet of sunflowers into Catherine's arms. The women crowded around her to offer congratulations, and she blushed and looked helplessly at Josh. See, see what they're doing to me? she asked silently.

She told the women it meant nothing, but they insisted. Magdalena had caught the bouquet at the last wedding, and look what happened. Catherine joined in the merriment, but she couldn't believe she'd be the next to marry. How could she when she had no one to marry? It had all been planned and orchestrated, no doubt by Jacinda.

Soon the guests dispersed into carts or onto horses for the ride to Doña Blanca's for the reception. Catherine invited as many villagers as could fit to ride with her in the truck. Old Pedro had brought his burro. Josh drove his car.

Next to Catherine sitting on the front seat was her neighbor Doña Maritza, holding Catherine's flowers in her lap. The back was filled with men from the mine, bunched together in their Sunday suits.

The talk was of the weather. Would it rain or would it not? If so, would it spoil the party? They needn't have worried. By the time the overloaded truck reached the large farmhouse of

Doña Blanca, the skies were clearing and the sound of a brass band warming up filled the air.

Josh slowed to a stop in front of the farmhouse and got out to join the party. After jumping down from the front seat, Catherine straightened her hat. She stood for a moment, watching the bright colors of the dresses and the dark suits as the guests mingled on the patio.

From the edge of the crowd Jacinda beckoned to both of them. "Today is a day to forget about work," she called, and ran to meet them. Taking Josh by one hand and Catherine by the other, she pulled them down the path to join the party. "It is a day to dance and eat and celebrate. You saw who caught the wedding bouquet," she confided to Josh with a wink. "We all know who will be the next to marry."

Josh nodded emphatically as if he agreed with her, and Catherine gave Jacinda a stern look.

"Tell her what you told me. That we don't have enough in common," Josh suggested.

"It won't do any good. She has her mind made up."

He shrugged. "Maybe she's right. Maybe we ought to do it their way. After all, they don't have as many divorces as we do."

"That's just what she told me the other day. Do you mean you'd be willing to marry someone Jacinda chose for you?"

He grinned. "Only because I know who she'd choose. You must admit she has good taste."

Catherine's head spun. "Good taste in choosing me or you?"

"Both of us. Maybe we deserve each other."

Jacinda's head turned from Josh to Catherine, trying to figure out if they were arguing or flirting. Finally she joined their hands together and took her place in the circle. The brass band began to play in earnest, a four-measure tune that was repeated over and over. Soon the whole group was holding hands and swaying to the music, a whirl of vibrant color, their pounding feet beating a rhythm that echoed inside Catherine's head.

When the dance was over, she was dizzy. Josh put his arm around her, and she relaxed against his side, fitting perfectly, the curve of her hip against his thigh. Jacinda appeared with cups of *chaca,* the fermented corn drink reserved for special occasions, then she waltzed away, her silver beads bouncing up and down on her chest. Catherine coughed as the drink burned a path down her throat. She sat down on a small bench.

"I should have known better," she said. "I've had it before. But not on an empty stomach."

"I'll get you something to eat," Josh said.

She nodded gratefully. "They're cooking a whole lamb around back. I'll wait here. That's men's territory."

Josh followed a cloud of smoke that billowed from the pit behind the house. One of the men, now in shirtsleeves, was turning the spit, the others watching and waiting their turn.

"If you marry for love and not money," Paco was saying, "you'll have good nights and bad days."

"In my opinion," one of the others said, "love is a ghost. Everyone talks about it, but few have seen it."

They all turned when Josh ambled up to survey the savory meat.

"Here is a banker," the groom said, his black tie slightly askew. "Let us ask his opinion. Is marriage the tomb of love?"

Josh shrugged. "I have never been married," he said slowly, "but I have heard that he who does not find love, finds nothing."

The men cheered loudly. Whether it was for the sentiment or that he'd constructed a whole sentence in Spanish, he didn't know. They cut him a slice of meat to try and he carried it in a napkin back to Catherine. But instead of Catherine Old Pedro was sitting on the bench.

Josh signaled to Pedro to wait while he went to his car to get the leather tool belt. He handed him the box as casually as he could. Pedro didn't speak when he saw the belt, but his eyes widened with surprise and pleasure. He buckled the belt around his waist and stood up to show Josh.

Just then Jacinda came up to admire Pedro's belt and the red rose in Josh's buttonhole. When he told her it came from Catherine, she smiled. "I believe," she said slowly, "that this is a match made in heaven."

Josh didn't tell Jacinda that he'd already heard all about it or that it was wishful thinking on her part. Weddings made people feel sentimental. It was the music, the flowers, and it was the *chaca*. He reached for his glass. Maybe a drink of *chaca* would make him a believer. He wanted to believe. He wanted to think there was room in his life for the luxury of falling in love, but he knew there wasn't. Not now. Not yet. Not until he was financially secure. Not until the fear of poverty had been erased from his mind.

When Josh didn't answer, Jacinda's face wrinkled into a hundred disappointed lines. She dusted off her skirt and headed for the long wooden table set up under the apple tree, taking Pedro with her. The bride and groom squeezed together at one end, and he saw Catherine beckon to him from the other side.

"Where were you?" he asked, taking his place next to her.

"In the kitchen helping the women. Where were you?"

"Talking with the men around the fire." He rested his hand lightly on the small of her back, feeling the heat from her skin through the thin fabric.

"About what?"

"You know. What men talk about." Laugh lines crinkled at the corners of his eyes.

"I don't know," she insisted, taking a piece of bread from a round basket.

He ran his hand up her spine. "Love and marriage."

"In Spanish?" she asked, suddenly breathless.

"Of course." He poured sparkling white wine into her glass. "What were you talking about in the kitchen?"

"Love and marriage."

"What did you hear?" he asked.

"The women think it's better for a woman to marry a man who loves her rather than a man she loves."

"That sounds like Jacinda," he said under his breath.

She shook her head. "Jacinda says to keep your eyes wide open before marriage and half shut afterward."

At the far end of the table the groom stood and raised his glass to his new wife.

"Now everyone makes a toast," Catherine explained, touching her glass to Josh's.

"I don't know any toasts, especially in Spanish," he said, a look of panic in his dark eyes. But when it was his turn he asked Catherine if she'd translate for him a poem he'd heard once. The guests leaned forward, hushed and expectant. His brain was clear despite the *chaca,* but his lips were numb and he wasn't sure they'd move.

"For those who love, time is eternity, hours fly, flowers die, new days, new ways, pass by. Love stays."

It didn't rhyme in Spanish, but they liked it, anyway. At least he thought they did. Jacinda came around behind him and kissed him on the cheek. Catherine looked thoughtful.

After dinner Doña Blanca asked Josh to lower the piñata from the cottonwood tree so the children could reach it. Catherine tied a bandanna over their eyes and put a stick in their hands. One by one they swung wildly, but no one was able to do more than graze it slightly. A ripple of laughter went through the crowd when Jacinda tied the bandanna over Catherine's eyes.

"Let's see if the *gringa* has any better luck," she said. Then she spun Catherine around until she reeled dizzily, her stick at her side, unable to get her bearings. Cautiously she raised her arm and completely by chance hit the papier-mâché donkey.

A resounding crack echoed through the air, and she felt the candy fall on her head and shower all around her. She could hear the excited cries of the children as they scrambled for the covered almonds. Fumbling with the knot on the bandanna, she felt someone else's fingers cover hers and untie it for her. The clean scent of his skin, the touch of his fingers gave him away.

Still dizzy, she put her hands on his shoulders to steady herself. When the bandanna fell away, she looked into his blue eyes, brimming with laughter.

"You did good, *gringa.* Surprised everybody."

"Including myself." The world continued to turn, and she hung on to Josh, the only constant in the crazy, spinning world. The shrieks of the children, the laughter of the adults and the music of the band all faded into the background and left them alone, just the two of them. They might have stood there forever in a trance if Jacinda hadn't tapped Catherine on the shoulder.

"I have spoken to him a little earlier," she said with a glance at Josh, "but I fear he did not understand my meaning. You must tell him that I believe you and he are meant for each other. And I am not the only one in this village who says that. Ask anyone."

Catherine stared at her. "You must be joking. I can't tell him that."

Jacinda tapped her toe impatiently. "What else must the man do? He dances, he recites poetry, he loans money. What more do you want?"

Catherine was speechless. It was a good question. What more did she want?

Josh smiled knowingly at Jacinda and put his arm around Catherine. When thunder rumbled in the distance, he looked up at the darkening sky. "I have to get back to town before the storm."

Jacinda shook her head disapprovingly. "It isn't safe for Señor Bentley to drive back tonight. And since it would not be proper for him to stay at your house unchaperoned, he can spend the night in my hayloft."

Josh stifled a groan. He understood the part about not driving back that night, and instantly his mind was filled with thoughts of spending the night with Catherine, either in her hammock or her bed. But Jacinda, who was usually on his side, had ruined that plan. And a good thing, too. All he needed was another test of his self-control.

"Tell her thanks for the invitation," he said. "But first I'll drive you home whenever the party's over."

Catherine smiled at a guitarist with ribbons hanging from his hat who strolled by. "The party won't be over until everyone falls into a stupor or tomorrow morning. Whichever comes first. I'll leave the truck here. I'm ready to go."

Before they left they gave their gifts to the newlyweds and thanked Jacinda, who gave Catherine a piece of the wedding cake to put under her pillow. "You will dream of the man you will marry," she promised with an elaborate wink.

Josh piloted Catherine to his car, and when Catherine glanced over her shoulder, she saw Jacinda at the edge of the patio, her hands on her hips, watching them.

Catherine sighed. "She's unbelievable. She's used this wedding to put pressure on me to get married. Honestly, it almost makes me want to go back to the land of the brave and the free. Where women can live beyond twenty-eight without getting hassled about being single."

He started the car. "You mean back to Tranquility?"

She leaned back. "No, no, not Tranquility. I couldn't bear to face the sight of condos and shopping centers on our land." The thought of her failure to keep the farm going made her flush with shame. She was glad it was too dark for him to see her face.

"Where will you go when your tour is up?" He drove slowly down the hill and turned up her road.

She pressed her hands to her cheeks to cool them. "I'm not sure. Wherever the Peace Corps sends me. Peru, Chile... Argentina. Wherever they need me. Coming here has been good for me. To see them succeed, to be a part of their success... It's almost as if it never happened."

"You mean losing the farm." He pulled up in front of her house and turned off the engine. "It must have been terrible."

"Not for everybody. My sister could hardly wait to leave the farm. And my parents have adjusted." She shook her head. "I don't know how."

"How they could adjust or how they could sell the farm?"

"Both." She paused. "I know, I know. They had no choice. But I...I..." She swallowed hard and a tear slid down her cheek. She turned her face to the window, but he took her by the shoulders to face him. She managed a half smile. "Sorry. It's not the farm. I'm over that. It must be the wedding."

He wiped the tear from her cheek with his thumb. "That's right. You cry at weddings."

Outside the rain began at last, sending streams down the windshield of Josh's car, creating a cocoon inside of warmth and security. She didn't want to get out and run through the rain to her house. Not by herself. She leaned back against the door. There was the faint smell from the crushed rose in Josh's buttonhole.

"You were a big hit with your dancing and offering your poem. I didn't know bankers liked poetry."

He pressed his knuckles together. "Tell me about bankers in Tranquility."

"They're boring. It's a boring story. You don't want to hear it."

"Yes, I do."

She sighed. "Well, there's old Mr. Grant and his son. They own the bank and they lend the money."

"To you?"

She drummed her fingers on her knee. "To us, to everybody. But when we needed them, they let us down." He didn't say anything. He waited for her to continue. "I guess I told you we were never rich. Whenever we came up short, we could always sell a sow or something. Until we ran out of live-stock."

"Do you blame the bank for that?"

She thought for a moment. "No, I blame myself, but they could have given us another chance." She clenched her hand into a fist. "Just one more loan for the next crop year. We might have made it. But my parents were tired. They didn't have the energy. They were relying on me and I was relying on them. I was their hope because I went to college and learned all about modern agriculture. But when it counted, I let them down." She pressed her hands to her cheeks. "They must have wondered what good it did me, my fancy education. Mr. Grant did. I could see it in his eyes when he turned me down the last time."

"Then what happened?"

"We sold the sheep and the grain and most of the machinery. Until there wasn't anything left except the land. And then the bank foreclosed. That doesn't surprise you, does it? You would have done the same."

"I suppose so. The bank's pockets are only so deep. You know the same thing will happen if you don't make the payments on your truck, don't you?"

"Of course," she said quickly. "We've been through that." She reached for the door handle behind her. The atmosphere had stopped being warm and cozy, and now felt stifling. She said good-night. It wasn't Josh's fault that the bank had foreclosed on her farm. It wasn't her parents' fault for trying to salvage enough for their retirement. She knew that, and yet the knot of resentment in her chest tightened whenever she thought about the land she'd lost. At least she'd learned a lesson. If she couldn't have her own farm, she'd use what she learned and devote her life to helping other farmers.

Impulsively she leaned forward and kissed Josh on the cheek, grabbed her wedding cake, opened the door before he could respond and ran through the rain to her front porch. She heard his door open and his footsteps behind her. By the time he reached the porch, his hair was plastered to his head, his strong features stood out even in the darkness. He pulled her toward him, crushing her breasts against his wet shirt. In an instant his mouth was on hers, tasting like rain and wine and wind.

She forgot the farm. She forgot everything they'd been talking about. All she could think of was how good it felt to lose herself in his kiss. The kiss deepened, lengthened, and she could no longer think at all.

Finally he broke off and held her at arm's length. "Jacinda could be right. Maybe we were meant for each other. Why don't you tell her we're thinking it over? Just to humor her."

Catherine wrapped her arms around her waist and shook her head. Drops of water fell from her dark hair to her shoulders. "I can't do that. She'd get her hopes up."

He ran his hand through her hair. "Her hopes? What about mine? What about yours?"

She started to tremble uncontrollably from the ups and downs of an emotional roller-coaster day.

Alarmed, Josh opened the door for her. "Get in before you catch pneumonia," he ordered. "And don't forget to put the cake under your pillow."

Inside she leaned against the door for support until she heard his car drive back to Jacinda's to spend the night in her hayloft. Then she opened the door and retrieved the piece of cake from the porch. After she showered, she put the cake under her pillow. She didn't believe in any of that superstitious nonsense, but she did it, anyway. Maybe it was the cake or maybe it wasn't, but she dreamed of Josh sleeping next to her in the hammock with the rain pouring down, soaking their clothes and then their skin until they melted together.

She woke up and reached for him. But she was in her bed and she was alone. The rain had stopped. The air was absolutely still except for the faint sound of a car in the distance. A car traveling the long road back to town, back to another world. His world.

Chapter Seven

When it was light, Catherine walked over to Doña Blanca's with a basket of fresh eggs over her arm to get the truck. The men who had stopped by to drink leftover *chaca* and bang pots and pans under the newlyweds' window were admiring the engine, the gleaming exterior and the extra-large tires.

Catherine handed over the keys to Manuel, the husband of Doña Blanca. She smiled as the children came running and piled into the long bed. The men took turns driving down the road, turning around and coming back again. One of them would drive to market on Monday, since they had the day off. Catherine would sit in back with the women, and the rest of the men would ride along and help unload. They were chattering excitedly about the trip to town, eager to pull up in front of the market in their own big, beautiful truck.

Catherine, too, was eager to pull up in front of the Rodriguez Market. Not that she expected to see Josh there, of course. But then why did her heart beat faster when they turned the corner of the cobblestone street where the policeman in his green uniform stood directing traffic?

Of course he wasn't there. He was probably still in bed, in his penthouse apartment overlooking the city. Or if he wasn't there he was already at work, in his high-rise office far above the smoke and the fumes and the noise. She looked up in the direction of the tall buildings that stood outlined in the early-morning light.

The atmosphere was different in the stall with the men around, lifting, carrying, laughing and joking. Sometime around midday Jacinda gave Catherine a series of sharp, inquisitive looks. Catherine gave her her best serene smile so she couldn't possibly guess that Catherine was suffering from postwedding blues. The kind that make you think the whole world was paired off while you longed for someone of your own.

She would be fine tomorrow when the men went back to work and things were back to normal. But her mind wandered back to the wedding. To the feeling of the rain on her skin and Josh's lips on hers. Her eyes wandered, too, searching among the crowds of shoppers for a tall figure with close-cropped dark hair who towered above the others. But he didn't come.

After lunch the crowds thinned out. Some of the women leaned back against the sacks of potatoes and closed their eyes. But Jacinda never rested. Her black eyes assessed Catherine, and she took her by the arm. "Let us go have a coffee and discuss business."

"Business?" Catherine asked. "So soon after the wedding?"

Jacinda nodded solemnly, but said no more until they were seated at the counter of Don Panchito's coffee shop.

"You know my friend Doña Margarita who made your new sweater and skirt?"

"Of course I do."

Jacinda lowered her voice. "She went to the bank to ask for a loan."

"Really? What happened?"

"Señor Bentley treated her very kindly and sent her to the loan counselor, the same one who teaches us. He gave her the forms to fill out and bring back today, but..." Jacinda paused and her eyebrows knit together in a frown. "They did not fill them out because they cannot write very well. I thought perhaps you . . ."

Catherine looked at her watch. "What time is the appointment?"

"Five o'clock," Jacinda said. "I didn't want to bother you, but they have no one else to ask."

Catherine set her cup down. "Of course I'll help if I can."

Jacinda's face wrinkled into a smile. "You can."

Making their way up the hill, Jacinda explained that Doña Margarita and her daughter and her son-in-law wanted the loan to buy alpaca sheep. With the softer wool they could make better sweaters and charge more.

While her daughter manned the stall, Margarita and Catherine pored over the papers in the back. When they finished, Margarita asked Catherine to go with them to the bank. They looked so nervous that she couldn't turn them down. In a few minutes she found herself on the familiar route across town and up the avenue. She was afraid Josh would be there. She was more afraid that he wouldn't.

Without him it would be all business. With him it could get emotional. What if he turned them down? After talking with Margarita, Catherine was convinced the group would make good use of the money and could earn enough to pay it back. It should be easy to see, but what if Josh didn't see it that way? What if she wasn't being objective? If she wasn't, Josh would let her know. That was what she was afraid of.

She needn't have worried. The loan officer Josh had assigned to them treated them with all the courtesy reserved for his most valued customers. When she saw they were at ease with him, Catherine slipped out of the office and stood in front of the elevator, watching the arrow above go as high as twelve. Twelfth floor, Josh's office. Hypnotically the arrow jerked its way downward, and when it stopped, the door opened and Josh got out.

She gulped. A surprised smile lit his face. "What are you doing here?" he asked, clasping her hands in his.

For a moment she was unable to speak. "I'm on my way home," she said at last, trying to ignore the vibrations set off by the touch of his hands.

He pulled her with him across the lobby. "I'm glad you caught me. I'm on my way home, too. My stove finally arrived with the rest of my stuff."

"I came with the weavers," she said, standing at the heavy glass doors with him. "They're in with Duran, the loan officer, talking about getting a loan so they can buy alpaca sheep."

"Have they got a support group, a decent profit margin and one year's experience?" he asked.

She nodded eagerly. "All that and more."

"Then they'll probably get it. But that's Duran's decision. Sometimes a group has everything on paper, but there's something that doesn't sit right. That's when a loan officer uses his intuition."

"I guess that's what you used when you decided to take a chance on us."

He looked thoughtful, but his thoughts weren't on their loan. "Would you like to come by and see my stove? It's brand-new with all the latest attachments."

"I really can't. The women are waiting for me." But she didn't go; she just stood there and watched him, waiting as if her shoes were made of lead and not canvas.

"Who would drive them home if you didn't?"

"I guess Miguel would, but . . ."

"Fine. I'll get someone to take a message. We'll go see my stove and then we'll go out to eat. I'll get you a taxi later. How's that?" he asked with a smile so dazzling she couldn't say no. She couldn't say anything at all.

Her stomach churned. Her knees knocked. Another evening with Josh Bentley. Another chance to feel his arms around her, his lips on hers. She ought to leave. Right now. But her doubts vanished with the wind as he caught her arm and they hurried down the steps onto the street.

Her feet, which had been leaden only moments ago, suddenly flew along the ground, keeping up with his. Together they negotiated the crowded sidewalks, edging around couples walking arm in arm and window shoppers, their faces pressed against the glass of smart shops. In front of the supermarket she paused.

"Instead of going out to dinner we could buy some groceries and initiate your stove," she suggested.

"Can you cook?"

"Can I cook?" she repeated incredulously. "Can chickens lay eggs? I can cook for barn raisings and church socials. I can cook for field hands and cornhuskers. I ought to be able to cook for one banker with both hands tied behind me."

"That won't be necessary," he said, the corners of his eyes crinkling with amusement. "I haven't had a real meal at home since I got here."

"Not that there's anything wrong with the food at your favorite restaurant," she said, pushing the door open. "But it will be interesting to see what they've got in here. A little market research on my part. Some comparative shopping."

He pushed the cart while she walked ahead, picking up cans and putting them back, frowning at prices and raising her eyebrows at the produce. She picked up a head of lettuce. "Shall we have a salad?"

"Sure." Suddenly self-conscious, he looked around at the other shoppers. "Have you seen any other men in here?" he asked in a loud whisper.

"I don't think so. In Aruaca only housewives go shopping. Men have better things to do."

"Like having a siesta on the couch, I'll bet. I'd rather be with you . . . in the supermarket. Since I don't have a couch."

She snapped some green beans between her fingers. "Day old," she whispered, and Josh rolled his eyes in dismay. "But we'll make do," she assured him, "with a little lemon juice and butter." Then she found the meat counter and told the butcher to wrap up two thick lamb chops.

Standing in line at the checkout counter, Catherine stood on tiptoe and whispered in Josh's ear. "The vegetables aren't as good as ours. And they're twice as expensive."

"But there's no bargaining. That's what I like."

She smiled, thinking of him standing in front of her with the mangoes in his hand, placing the money in her palm. Still feeling the touch of his fingers as he closed her hand and held it tightly. Remembering how the sounds of the market had faded around her. There was no shouting in this supermarket, no gleeful cries or arguments over the prices.

Josh paid the clerk and carried the groceries in one hand, using the other to link with Catherine's as he led her through the streets to his apartment. While they waited to cross the street, he tapped his heel against the pavement impatiently. He wanted to see her reaction to his apartment. He tried to picture her there with her wide skirts and her hat and her braid. Could she fit into his life? Would she want to? Probably not. And whatever he wanted he had no right to draw her into his life. There was no place for her or for dreams. He needed to become more secure before he could forget about his poor, lonely childhood and make plans for his future. He'd have to wait. *She'd* have to wait. Josh made himself control his growing feelings. Now wasn't the time for them.

They took the elevator up to the penthouse. He unlocked the door, and she stood in the doorway and stared out across the pale carpet to the breathtaking view of Teregape with the last rays of sun on it.

"It's beautiful," she said breathlessly. She slipped out of her shoes, stepped over a cardboard box and went to the window. He opened the sliding glass door, and she walked out to the balcony. Standing behind her, he remembered seeing it for the first time, that incredible view. He lifted her hat from her head and set it on the table. His fingers itched to loosen her braid and see her hair cascade to her shoulders.

Finally she looked around. "You don't have any furniture. It looks as if no one lives here."

"I have a stove," he protested. "And a bed. The essentials. And we could really do without the stove."

She stifled a smile. Her gaze turned to the boxes stacked in the corner. "What's in those?"

"I don't know. I can't remember. I packed so long ago. They must have come by sea with the refrigerator. By the time I get around to unpacking, it will be time to pack up again."

Startled by the thought of Josh leaving, she smoothed the hair that strayed from the edges of her braid. "You mean you're not staying... I thought..."

He shrugged. "I don't know. I'm up for a promotion. I guess I mentioned that. If I get it, I'll go back to Boston and they'll send someone to replace me here. I don't know when it'll come or if it'll come. If it does, I'll have to pack up and go. They told me not to get too attached to anything I couldn't bring back in my suitcase." His eyes traveled the length of her body as if he were measuring to see if she'd fit.

She felt the heat course through her body until she would have bet she could have been melted down and packed in an overnight bag. She tore her gaze from his and looked around desperately. "I haven't seen the . . . uh . . ."

"The bed?"

"The stove."

"Right in here."

In the compact kitchen she ran her hand over the smooth ceramic surfaces, opened the broiler and examined the grill. She turned on the oven, then washed the lettuce, relieved to have something to do with her hands and something to think about except Josh's leaving. She shook the lettuce leaves so vigorously that Josh held up his hands in self-defense.

"I was just thinking about taking a shower," he said.

"Uh-huh," she said absently, and watched him disappear down the hall. It was like playing house, cooking in this little kitchen with its shiny new appliances. When he came back, he'd showered and changed into his blue jeans and a striped T-shirt. When he shed his suit, he seemed to shed some of the stiffness she always associated with bankers. Although there had been nothing stiff about the way he looked at her on the balcony.

He sniffed appreciatively at the smell of lamb sprinkled with rosemary that wafted through the air. The room was filled with steam from the green beans simmering in a pot. He closed his eyes and wrapped his arms around her. The smell of his clean shirt made her want to bury her face against his chest. His voice sunk to a low rumble.

"So this is what I've been missing at the restaurant."

His cheek was next to hers, his hair damp. She lifted her hands to his shoulders.

He pulled her close. She had a glimpse of longing in his eyes, the same longing that threatened to engulf her. Added to the steam and the smoke in the air there was desire. She stood still, afraid to move, afraid to break the spell. It was the oven timer that did it with its shrill ring, and they broke apart.

"We'll eat on the balcony," he said, taking a bottle of wine from a rack on the counter and two glasses from the cupboard. She followed him with plates of food. Dusk was falling and the lights of the city sparkled below. He saw the sight every night, and yet he felt as if he'd never seen it before. He stole a look at Catherine, her profile so perfect that he felt a lump in his throat.

They ate in silence, watching the sky change from navy to blue-black. He left her there while he made coffee, and when he returned, she had her head tilted back against the wrought-iron chair.

"You're right," she said, taking the cup from him. "You can't make out the constellations from here."

"No," he agreed. "Your hammock's the best place to be."

She didn't answer. It was clear neither of them would ever forget that night. "I've forgotten where the Southern Cross is."

He set his cup down. "I should get my telescope."

"Where is it?" she asked lazily. She felt her bones turn to jelly. She was totally relaxed, totally happy gazing out at the city below with Josh at her side, saying nothing, just knowing he was there. It was odd. Here she was far from home under an unfamiliar sky with a man she scarcely knew, and yet she felt a strange sense of belonging that caught her by surprise.

She, who hated the city, felt uneasy in crowds and detested bankers, had come to a high rise in the middle of a big city with a bona fide banker, kicked off her shoes and cooked dinner for him. And was having the best time she'd had in years. She reminded herself that all it was was play. They were both playing a game, knowing that everything here was temporary. They were in a different hemisphere, everything was turned upside down and anything seemed possible. Only it wasn't, not really. One day he'd go away and she would, too. But not yet. Not quite yet.

Reluctantly she left the dark balcony and followed Josh to the living room where he snapped on the lights and ripped open the top of the first carton. She knelt next to him, looking at the clothes on top and the books on the bottom. Books on economics and books on banking, but no telescope.

Wrapped in felt was a framed diploma from a university outside Boston. Catherine whistled under her breath. "No wonder you're such a good banker. You have all the right credentials. And you read all the right books." She leaned back against the wall, sinking into the soft, thick carpet.

"I don't know why I brought that diploma along. I thought I'd hang it in my office."

She drew her knees to her chin, her long skirt covering her legs. Undoing her braid, she shook her hair loose. "Where did you get the funds to go to that school if your father blew all his money chasing rainbows?"

"Scholarship." He opened the next box. More clothes and a can of baked beans and a tin of brown bread. He looked up with a sheepish grin. "Emergency rations."

At the bottom he found a framed photograph wrapped in cotton batting. As he unwrapped it, she moved to his side and rested her chin on his shoulder. It was an old black-and-white picture taken at the entrance to a cave. A group of Indians leaned on shovels and stared seriously at the camera. In the center was a young man smiling proudly, binoculars around his neck and a pick in one hand.

"My father," he explained after a long silence. "At the Tochabamba Mine."

She exhaled softly. "So it really does exist."

He shook his head. "No, it doesn't. It's a dream."

She pointed to the picture. "Then how...?"

"The mine was real. The silver wasn't. It was low-grade ore from what I can figure. Fool's silver. And right there is one of the biggest fools who ever spent his last dollar on shares in a silver mine." He clamped his lips together and shook his head. "So even if there hadn't been an avalanche, it wasn't worth the effort."

"Are you sure you don't want to go there, just to see—"

"Yes. Old Pedro is right. If the God of Thunder closed the mine, he must have had a good reason. We have no right to disturb it."

She thought for a long moment, then ran her finger around the frame of the picture. "You should hang it on the wall, as a reminder..."

"A reminder of what not to do with your life? I don't think so. Growing up without money is bad enough. Growing up without a father is even worse."

"Then why did you bring it with you?"

He lay flat on the floor and stared up at the ceiling, his arms folded under his head, the telescope forgotten. "I don't know."

She studied the photograph. "There's a resemblance there, something in the eyes..."

"Between him and me? Uh-uh. We couldn't be more different."

Catherine studied Josh's face. The overhead light emphasized the tight muscles in his neck and the lines in his forehead. Maybe he didn't know why he'd brought the picture. Maybe he didn't recognize the dreamer in himself. But she saw it in his eyes and heard it in his voice.

"Catherine." He didn't move from his prone position on the floor, but there was a note of urgency in his voice. "What do you want? What are you looking for?"

She didn't hesitate. "I'm not looking for anything. I've found it. My life is helping farmers help themselves. The fates and the weather and the bank took my farm away from me, but they gave me a chance to use what I learned in other ways. It's taken me a long time to see it that way, but now I think this was my destiny all along."

"You believe in fate?"

"Yes, but I also believe in making plans. Right now I have a five-year plan."

He rolled over onto his side and squinted up at her. "Tell me about it."

"Well, after I finish out my term here, I'm going to re-up. I want to stay in South America, since I've spent all this time learning Spanish, and I want to go someplace where they're having problems, where they need me."

"You need to be needed, don't you?"

"Even more than that I need to be successful, to see some tangible results of my work. But there's nothing new about that. Everyone feels that way." She stretched her legs out in front of her. It was time to stop talking about herself. It was time to leave. She had to go before it was too late. While she still had the will to break the spell of this evening. "Enough about me. I really have to go." She said it, but she didn't move. What was wrong with her?

He propped his chin on his elbow. "You can't leave yet. You haven't seen the rest of the apartment."

"You mean the bedroom."

"Yes, it's got a great big bed and a view, too."

"I'm sure it's spectacular."

"It is," he assured her. "Especially in the morning."

"Maybe some other time," she said, ignoring the unspoken invitation. Move, she told herself. Get up off the floor and go, but still she stayed.

"When will that be?"

"I don't know. We wouldn't want to make this a habit." A habit of coming home and cooking dinner and going to bed in the big bed down the hall and waking up to a spectacular view and Josh. She wrapped her arms around her waist to keep from trembling.

"I understand. Too much work. Next time I'll do the dinner."

"I didn't know you could cook. Besides your favorite restaurant would start to miss you."

"They'll have to get along without me sooner or later."

And so would she, she thought. So would she. And just when she finally summoned the courage to stand up, he reached for her and pulled her into his arms. She shouldn't have let him mold her body to his. She shouldn't have returned his kisses, but his lips were soft and his kisses so achingly sweet that she couldn't stop.

He took her face in his hands and brushed her cheeks with his strong, warm fingers. His eyes were full of wonder and his voice was unsteady. "I can't let you go."

Her breath caught in her throat. If she didn't go now, she never would. She stood, her knees threatening to give way.

He got to his feet and put his arms around her. He couldn't let her go, but he had to. Just one more kiss, he told himself. One more chance to lose himself in the depths of those dark eyes. Eyes that could be so earnest one moment and so dreamy the next. She thought he looked like his father. She thought he should go to the mine. She couldn't be more wrong. Didn't she know it was ridiculous to spend time and money searching for a worthless hole in the ground hidden God knows where?

Her lips were soft, as red and ripe and irresistible as the berries that grew in her garden. He lowered his mouth to hers. Her hands clung to his shoulders as he held her tightly against his chest. Unable to stop, unable to resist one more taste, one more kiss. He felt his caution dissolve. If he allowed himself a dream, it would be to hold her like this, to bury himself in the warmth of her body, to make her his for one night. But he fought it off, the dream and the desire and the longing.

He dropped his arms, and she looked up in surprise. Hadn't he said that he couldn't let her go? Hadn't he kissed her as though there were no tomorrow? Bewildered, she stepped back and found her shawl draped over the kitchen counter. "I really must be going," she said, and this time he didn't protest.

They stood in front of the apartment building waiting for a taxi, and when it came, he closed the door and watched her go.

Catherine closed her eyes in the taxi, but she couldn't sleep. She'd get over Josh, but it wasn't going to be easy. She had to start now. She couldn't wait until he left. It would hurt too much. She liked him. She liked him too much. She saw that under his caution and conservative good judgment there was the soul of a dreamer. He'd never admit it, but it was there. It might surface one day, but she wouldn't be around to see it.

She told herself theirs was a case of opposites attracting. And how they attracted, she thought, still feeling the aching longing in her body. This was a case of two people who never should have met and never should have given in to their feelings. She was looking to help people and he was looking for a promotion. They both knew it. It was time to taper off gradually until she hardly noticed she wasn't seeing him anymore.

Maybe it would be best to quit cold turkey. But the thought of never seeing him again made her head pound. She pressed her hand against her head, but the pounding wouldn't stop. And the dreams of Josh made her sleep restless.

The next morning she leaned out her bedroom window, trying to decide what to do, when she saw Old Pedro looking up at her, his burro tethered to a tree.

Rubbing her eyes, she told him she'd be right down. She dressed quickly in her old jeans and work shirt and hurried to the door. He tipped his hat, declined her invitation to come in for coffee, but sat on the chair on her front porch and slowly looked around. Then he patted the tool belt Josh had given him, which he was wearing around his waist.

She nodded. She sat in the other chair and asked Pedro if he thought it would rain. He shook his head, tilted his sombrero and looked around. It occurred to Catherine that he might be looking for Josh.

"The *señor* isn't here," she said. "The one who wanted to go to the mine. He lives in La Luz."

"If you see him, tell him I have changed my mind."

Catherine's eyes widened. "But why?"

"I had a dream," he explained. "I dreamed the *padrón* came to me and asked me to take *el señor* banker to the mine."

Catherine leaned forward. "Are you no longer afraid?"

He nodded. "I am afraid. But the *padrón* said to me the danger is over. The God of Thunder has moved elsewhere, but the treasure remains. He told me to divide the treasure among the children and grandchildren of those who perished in the mine, and the *señor*, of course. For them I will go one last time."

Catherine bit her lip. How could she tell him Josh didn't want to go to the mine? She couldn't explain that Josh wasn't interested in taking risks. So she promised Pedro she would give Josh the message and watched him ride away on his burro until he disappeared in the dust. She promised to give him the message, but she didn't say when.

Chapter Eight

On the next market day Catherine was behind the wheel once more. The men had gone back to the mines and the women were subdued. In the back of the truck they were feeling their own postwedding blues. Still they did a good business and at the end of the day packed their cash in cloth bags. Catherine took Jacinda aside and told her she was going to wait for them in the truck.

Jacinda's eyes narrowed. "It is not safe to wait alone at this time of day," she warned.

"Then I'll wait in Don Panchito's coffee shop. Is that safe enough?"

Jacinda folded her arms across her blue apron. "Why do you not come with us? Señor Bentley will be disappointed."

"No, he won't," she said firmly. "Señor Bentley doesn't care who brings the money. This is business. Besides, I'm tired."

Jacinda snorted. "What is wrong with you, Catalina? I see sadness, not tiredness in your face. And now you will not come to the bank. What am I to tell Señor Bentley?"

Catherine threw her hands into the air. "Tell him I have a strange disease. I don't care what you tell him."

Jacinda's mouth fell open in surprise at this outburst. Glancing over her shoulder, she saw the women had gone ahead, and she lifted her skirts and hurried after them without another word to Catherine. Heaving a sigh, Catherine walked to the coffee shop, relieved to be out from under the scrutiny of Jacinda's sharp eyes.

She slid onto a stool at the counter, and Don Panchito filled a small cup of hot coffee for her. Gratefully she sipped her coffee, satisfied that she had avoided a meeting with Josh. But her satisfaction didn't last long. Someone scraped the legs of the stool next to her across the concrete floor.

Out of the corner of her eye she saw Josh sit down next to her and order an espresso. He didn't say anything, so they sat there drinking their coffee, acutely aware of each other, without speaking.

Finally he broke the silence. "I hear you're suffering from a rare disease," he remarked.

"Don't worry. It's not contagious," she assured him.

"Good. Let's have dinner. I need to talk to you."

"I can't. This doesn't make sense, you know."

He turned to face her. "What?"

"Us seeing each other. We're far from home. We're lonely, even homesick. It's natural that we seek out each other's company, but..." Funny how she had it all worked out in her mind, and now that he was here, sitting next to her, she couldn't remember what she was going to say.

"Very natural," he said smoothly.

"But not very professional. I'd feel better if we had a business relationship." Yes, that was it, a business relationship. How could he argue with that?

"So would I," he agreed. "In fact, that's why I'm here."

She blinked. "It is?" His agreeing with her so readily disarmed her.

"Yes, I need some help with a loan application."

"But I thought you didn't handle loans except..."

"Except on rare occasions. That's right. But this is a cousin of Duran's who's a fisherman on Lake Cordillera. He heard we were making small loans to small businesses. They want a motorboat to improve their catch. Duran would handle it, but that's a conflict of interest, so I volunteered. It's his cousin, after all. He shouldn't be discriminated against just because Duran works in the bank."

Other customers paid for their coffee and left. Catherine looked at Josh. "What does that have to do with me?"

"Nothing, except I need a translator and somebody to give a frank opinion of the situation."

"I can tell you right now I'm in favor of their getting the loan."

He set his cup down. "Without even seeing the operation?"

"Well . . . I suppose it would help."

"Then you'll come with me, as a favor to the bank, as a favor to the fishermen."

She smiled. "If you put it that way."

"Have you ever been there before?"

"To the highest lake in the world and the center of the Inca civilization? No, I've never been there before." And she really shouldn't go now, business or not. Yet those fishermen needed a spokesperson, someone who would understand and sympathize with their situation. She imagined standing on the shore of the lake, watching the sun reenact the Inca legend. A shiver ran down her spine at the thought. But was it the thought of the lake or sharing the experience with Josh that made her skin tingle in anticipation?

She dragged her eyes from his and stared into her coffee. "How would we get there?" she asked, knowing she'd already made up her mind.

"Take the train from Castillo."

Her heart leaped. A train ride through the high Andes. A trip she'd always wanted to take with a man who could make sharing a cup of coffee exciting. She wrapped her hands around her cup. "I suppose I could get away for a few days," she said slowly.

"Good." His eyes gleamed as he took her hand and they walked out the door together. They walked through the darkness toward the truck without speaking. When they reached the truck, he trailed his hand along her shoulder in a caress.

"Drive carefully," he said. "I'll pick you up next Wednesday morning at your house."

The days seemed to drag until Wednesday. Josh didn't come to the market and she didn't go to the bank. She hadn't told Josh about Old Pedro changing his mind yet. She was afraid he'd say no again, even though deep down he wanted to go to the mine. Even more important, he *needed* to go there. But she knew he had to make that decision himself. Even as she paced back and forth on her front porch Wednesday morning while a light rain fell around her, she debated with herself the wisdom of telling him about Old Pedro.

Josh pulled up in front of her house with the rain falling. He couldn't believe she was there on the porch waiting for him. It was amazing that he'd convinced her to come along on this trip. If only she were going because of him. But he couldn't let himself believe that. Instead, she was going because she wanted to see the lake and because she wanted to help the fishermen get their loan.

Even so he was afraid she'd change her mind, so he'd avoided her this past week so she wouldn't have the opportunity to tell him she had to plant potatoes or pick berries or anything else rather than go with him. But with this rain he didn't see how anyone could do much planting of anything.

Before he could get out of his car she dashed through the light rain in her pink shirt that matched her cheeks and her khaki pants and jacket. Her hair, brushed back behind her ears, made her look about eighteen. When his eyes reached her sandaled feet, he frowned.

"I hope you brought some warm shoes. It's cold up there." He didn't tell her that if she hadn't he'd take her bare feet in his hands and warm them himself. He tore his eyes from her pink toes and started the car.

She adjusted her seat belt. "I know all about the lake," she told him, her smile sending excitement simmering through his body. He hadn't realized how much he'd missed seeing her this past week, or how much he wanted to take her in his arms and kiss her, right here in front of her house before they'd gone even one mile. But he started driving and she started talking about the Indians and their sun god. There was something about her voice that made everything she said sound fascinating.

She turned to face him, her eyes dark pools of mystery. "No one knows where the Incas came from," she said. "Legend has it they first appeared on the island in the middle of the lake, sent there by the sun god to start a new civilization." She gazed off dreamily at the white stone houses that lined the streets of Castillo. "I want to see the sun rise from the Island of the Sun the way they did, from the doorway of the temple."

Josh wanted to see the sun rise from the island, too, and he wanted to see it set with her. He didn't know what made him think of that. He'd convinced himself and her, too, that this was just a business trip. Now here he was wondering how she'd look with the early-morning sun on her face. It must be the legend of the Incas, one man and one woman, set down in the middle of a lake to begin civilization, that had set him off.

Lost in his thoughts, he drove past the train station, made a U-turn and doubled back.

"You know they say they submerged their treasure in the middle of the lake to hide it from the Spaniards." Catherine's tone was reflective, almost dreamy.

He parked the car next to the station and lifted their overnight bags from the back seat. He didn't speak until they were settled comfortably in the buffet car of the narrow-gauge train.

"You know," he said, looking out the window, "I've heard enough sunken treasure stories to last a lifetime. Usually there's just enough truth in them to send men off with their last dollar and a gleam in their eye."

She leaned forward in her seat. "Like your father?"

"Yes." The train started with a jolt, and he braced himself against the padded seat. "The last time I saw him he was going to look for sunken treasure off the coast of Mexico. He'd invested his last dollar in a recovery operation. All he had left except for the shares to the mine. And he would have sold those if he could have found someone to buy them. My mother kissed him goodbye as she always did and wished him good luck. But his luck had run out. His plane went down." His words were flat and emotionless, but underneath there was a current of regret and sadness.

Catherine laced her fingers together. "At least he left you something. A legacy. Something of his own. Something he valued."

"The shares to the silver mine? He left them to me because he couldn't sell them. They were worthless."

"Maybe, but my parents left me nothing. No house, no land . . . nothing."

"Nothing? What about the memories? The security of knowing you'd never go hungry, two parents there when you needed them, the barn with the hay and the kittens. All that."

She nodded slowly. "Yes, all that. Gone. Do you want to see where they live now?" She fished in her purse for her wallet and pulled out a snapshot of a man and a woman standing on a patio, a small postage-stamp lawn in the background.

"What's wrong with that?" he asked, holding the picture by the edges.

"It's a condominium," she explained patiently.

"You make it sound like a slum," he noted.

"You didn't see the farm," she said, her dark eyes reproachful.

He looked at the picture again. He could see where Catherine had gotten her dark, expressive eyes and her smile. "They look happy," he remarked.

"I know what you're thinking. If they're happy, why can't I be happy for them? I don't know. I feel like an ungrateful child." She sighed and put the picture back in her wallet.

He studied her face. "Maybe when you get back you'll feel differently about them."

She looked up sharply. "I'm not going back."

"That's right, too many memories," he said soothingly.

"Or not enough," she said, gazing intently out the window at the green-terraced hills and jagged white-capped mountains in the background.

The steward rang a little bell and took orders for lunch. After they ate, they talked about the descendants of the Incas they were going to visit. No further mention was made of buried treasure or lost farmland.

In the last hour they fell into a comfortable silence, watching rain clouds obscure the view, lulled into serenity by the gentle motion of the train. Catherine leaned back on the plush upholstery and closed her eyes. She wondered if there was anyone she'd rather be with than Josh on a train trip. Even though he couldn't possibly understand how she felt about the farm, there was a warmth in his gaze and sympathy she could wrap around her like a blanket. He cared about her, she realized suddenly. He really cared.

She stole a glance at him from under her lashes. He was looking at her with such longing that it made her heart contract. Why had he really brought her along on this trip? Did he only need a translator? And why had she come? Was it truly to see the Island of the Sun? Or was it that she'd go anywhere he went, just to be with him.

The train chugged to a stop before she could answer her own question. A railway spur ran directly to the lakefront pier where they got out to board the wind-powered ferry across the lake. Gulls swooped and cried in the late-afternoon sky. They looked out across the choppy sea.

"This is a long way to go to make a small loan, isn't it?" she asked.

He leaned against the railing of the boat. "I could have asked them to come to town to fill out the applications, but I wanted to see how they work and live and hear them tell me how they'd use the money."

She turned to look at him. "The way you did with us."

The wind blew his dark hair across his forehead. "I learned a lot by coming to the farm." He'd learned what caused the sadness in the depths of her eyes, and why she was afraid to fail, afraid even to return to the land where she'd failed.

She turned her collar up against the wind. The other passengers went inside the small cabin, and they were alone on the deck. "You never told me what made you change your mind."

Flecks of light glinted in his dark blue eyes, and he braced himself against the rise and fall of the boat. He knew what he couldn't say. He couldn't mention the hammock, or the night under the stars with her. "Maybe it was the way you talked to the potatoes," he said finally. "That's when I knew you were different from everybody else."

One corner of her mouth curved upward. "I hope you haven't told anyone about that. It's my secret method."

He grinned. A vicious wave slapped the side of the ferry, and he grabbed her arms to catch her as she pitched forward. His arms tightened around her. "Your secret is safe with me," he murmured in her ear. "And so are you." He pulled her back against the hull and crushed her to him. Their lips met and he kissed her with breathtaking thoroughness. She felt her knees weaken as the boat whistle announced their arrival.

Josh put his hands over her ears to protect them from the sharp whistle. Then he gently kissed Catherine's eyelids and the spot where her pulse fluttered at her temples. People were gathering their belongings and coming out on deck, but he ignored them. Instead he cupped her chin in his hands and lost himself in the depths of her dark eyes.

Her arms wound around him, and she reached up to thread her fingers in his short-cropped hair. He wished he knew what she was thinking. He'd given her two good reasons to come on this trip, translating for him and helping the villagers, but the look in her eyes made him hope there was another, more personal reason she'd come.

Over her head he saw that the boat had entered the lagoon. He wished they could sail around the lake all day with the wind in their hair and his lips on hers. Beneath the surface of her warm skin he felt the warmth of her heart, her generosity and her adventurous spirit. It was that he wanted to capture, to make part of himself. But somewhere in the distance was the last call, and she broke away, grabbed her bag and led him to the gangway.

Catherine smoothed her jacket and looked around at the reed boats that lined the shore without seeing them. She wondered if she looked as shaky as she felt. They hadn't even set foot on the island and already she was wondering how she would keep her feelings in check with Josh around. First she'd been oblivious to the arrival of the boat; now she didn't know which way to turn. Everyone on shore was yelling and waving to someone debarking.

Finally a short dark-haired man with high cheekbones approached them and introduced himself as Duran's cousin Miguel. Proudly he led them to the center of the island where twenty or so huts made of dried reeds clustered around a one-room schoolhouse of galvanized iron sheets. Men, women and barefoot children gathered to meet them, smiling shyly.

Miguel apologized for the scarcity of accommodations and asked if they would mind sleeping in the schoolhouse. Catherine shot Josh a nervous glance and said they'd be delighted.

After setting their bags inside the room filled with wooden benches, Miguel left them with instructions to come to his house for dinner. One light bulb swung from the ceiling, illuminating walls covered with students' pictures, and in the corner two straw mattresses were covered with clean sheets and blankets. The mattresses were placed a few feet apart, as if their hosts weren't exactly sure what their relationship was. They weren't the only ones, Catherine thought, directing her gaze to the small sink in the corner and the door that led to the bathroom.

She was trying so hard to keep her distance from Josh. She'd been doing so well until she stumbled against him on the deck. He said she was safe with him. But she knew that wasn't true. Nobody could keep someone else safe. Your only protection was to rely on yourself, then if you failed you could only blame yourself.

Josh walked around the room restlessly, picking up books and putting them down, then peering out the window into the rapidly falling night. Catherine leaned against the teacher's desk at the front of the room, trying not to look at the beds in the corner, trying not to think about sleeping next to Josh on a straw mattress.

Finally she ran out of places to look and her gaze caught Josh's and held. She thought of the intensity of his kisses on the boat deck, and tension filled the air in the schoolhouse. Maybe he was thinking about them, too. How on earth were they going to hang on to the last shred of their self-control while sleeping next to each other?

As if he'd read her thoughts, he leaned against the blackboard and cleared his throat. "What do you think of the sleeping arrangements? I hope you're not allergic to straw."

"No," she said. "What about you?"

He shook his head.

"On the other hand," she said, "it's a little stuffy in here. I'll move my mattress over to the window."

"Good idea." Before she could protest he was shoving both mattresses across the floor and wedging them together without a space between them.

Her brain spun with images of the length of her body pressed against his, his breath on her cheek, falling asleep in the warmth of his arms. "This *is* a business trip, isn't it?" she asked slowly, her eyes troubled.

"Of course," he said, as if he didn't know she was referring to the sleeping arrangements and the growing sexual tension between them. "I just haven't brought up the subject of the loan yet. I'm waiting for them to say something. But you know more about village etiquette. That's why you're so useful. That's why I brought you."

His blue eyes were clear and guileless. Useful, he said, like a calculator or an automatic teller machine. She felt foolish. He only put his mattress next to hers to enjoy the fresh air coming in through the window.

"What do you think?" he continued, lowering himself to the edge of the straw mattress. "Am I supposed to bring up the loan or are they?"

"Well, uh...I guess it's better to just wait," she concluded.

He rubbed his hands together briskly and stood. "That's settled. Let's go to dinner. They're expecting us."

Josh watched Catherine bend over the child-size sink to wash her hands. Her dark hair tumbled forward across her cheek. Despite his easy assurance he was having a hard time concentrating on the purpose of this trip. He was stuck on this island, trying to pretend every fiber of his being wasn't crying out for her.

What had possessed him to bring her here with him, then kiss her on the boat and now move his mattress next to hers?

He might be able to sleep in the same room as her, but how could he sleep next to her where he could see the moonlight shining on her hair, smell the scent of the soap on her skin, and not gather her into his arms? He had told himself not to move both mattresses, but somehow the message had gotten lost between his brain and his hands.

This whole trip was turning into a shambles because he couldn't stop thinking about Catherine. About how to get closer to her, physically and emotionally. No matter how close he got, it wasn't enough. He wanted to explore her body, every inch of it, and he wanted to know what was in her mind, every corner of it.

When he looked up, she was standing at the door, watching him and waiting. He gave her a reassuring smile and patted her on the back casually as she walked ahead of him, keeping his hand pressed to the small of her back as they crossed the clearing.

She paused to admire the llama tethered next to Miguel's house. She stroked its soft fur. "I wish I had one of these. They carry huge loads and have sweet dispositions."

Josh watched her lay her cheek against the soft fur of the animal's neck. "I'll get you one."

She shook her head. "Where would I keep it?"

His hand met hers on the llama's back. Her fingers were warm and her touch sent vibrations up his arm. "In the field behind your house."

"I mean, when I leave. What would we do—ride off into the sunset together, my llama and I?"

His eyes traced the outline of her lips, the shape of her eyebrows. "It would be quite a sight," he admitted. "But maybe you'd better wait until you get a farm of your own."

She stiffened and pulled her hand away. "I'm not going to get a farm of my own. If I don't own anything, I won't have anything to lose."

He opened his mouth to protest this philosophy, but just then the door of the hut swung open and Miguel beckoned to them. He seated them around a small table where they ate fresh fish with wheat cakes. After dinner Miguel's wife got out her knitting. Catherine watched while Miguel's young son wove a toy boat out of reeds.

A knock on the door signaled the arrival of the neighbors. They filed in, taking places on the floor and finally occupying every inch of space on the straw mats that covered the dirt.

Seated on the floor with the others and pressed tightly against Josh, she was conscious of the muscles in his arms, the fresh smell of the lake that clung to his clothes. While she studied the faces around the fire, wind-burned, weathered and lined with creases, she translated what the villagers said. As it turned out, they went straight to the subject of the loan.

"They say the reed boats are like wild horses. Hard to control. If they have motorboats, they can go smoother and farther and catch more fish."

"Who will they sell the extra fish to?" Josh asked.

"A big company is opening a cannery on the lake, and they'll buy all the fish they can catch. Trout were released in the lake some years ago, and they've grown beyond all expectations. They say they're huge." The men nodded and held out their arms to show how big they were.

"Tomorrow," they said, "you will see." Then they trooped out of the hut with promises to meet at dawn the next day to take Josh and Catherine out on the lake. Thanking Miguel and his wife for the dinner, Catherine and Josh strolled to the shore to look at the boats before retiring to the schoolhouse.

The night air was cool and soft on Catherine's skin. After sitting cross-legged in the small hut, her muscles ached to stretch out. At the edge of the lake she paused. A full moon appeared from behind the clouds and flooded the lake with its brilliance. She gasped. It looked like a pool of silver. From behind her she heard Josh's sharp intake of breath.

"Silver," he said, echoing her thoughts. "No wonder it drives men crazy." He put his hands on her shoulders and pulled her back against his chest.

She leaned against him, savoring the warmth of his body, feeling his heart pound. Was he thinking of the mine? Should she tell him Pedro had agreed to take him there? She didn't want to spoil this moment if he said no. This magic moment when the lake turned to liquid silver and her body felt like liquid fire.

She turned and he saw her face, pale as alabaster in the moonlight, tilted up to his. He struggled with the passion that raced through his body. He wanted to make love to her under the silver moon. If he kissed her now, he wouldn't be able to stop. Her eyes told him she wanted it too, but how would she feel in the morning in the cold light of day when he went back to being a banker in line for a promotion and she was a farmer without a farm?

Reluctantly he took her hand, and they walked single file back to the schoolhouse. She didn't speak and he sensed her disappointment, or was that wishful thinking? Maybe she was relieved. She changed into her nightgown in the bathroom. He caught a glimpse of pink fabric like spun sugar, and he remembered the nightgown hanging from the wall in her bedroom. The one she'd worn the night in the hammock.

He lay down with his clothes on and pretended to be asleep when she came out. When he heard the straw rustle on the mattress next to him, he didn't open his eyes. But he knew how she would look with her curves barely concealed, the sheer material grazing the tips of her breasts, and he turned over and buried his face in the flat pillow.

He heard her whisper good-night to him, but he didn't answer. His throat was clogged with desire. How much could a man take?

At dawn the fishermen knocked on their door, and Josh leaped off his mattress and went outside with them to drink strong coffee while Catherine got dressed. He'd slept fitfully, visions of Catherine in her nightgown coming and going, but never staying long enough to take hold of. Just like real life. He saw the men look at him with curious glances. Were they trying to decide what to think of his relationship with Catherine? He couldn't help them there. Half the time he didn't know what to think of it, either.

He smiled and talked to the men and drank coffee, but his eyes were on the door of the schoolhouse until she finally came out wearing a red sweatshirt and tan pants. Among the reeds she stood out like an exotic flower. Her cheeks shone as if she'd scrubbed them in the small sink, and her brown eyes sparkled in the early-morning light. The men offered her coffee and a chunk of bread, then they all went down to the shore.

They pushed off in separate canoe-shaped balsas before Josh had a chance to say anything more than good morning to her. Her boat dipped and bobbed while Josh watched nervously. He saw her grab the edge of the balsa as she leaned forward to speak to the fishermen.

"We paddle gently so as not to awaken the sleeping goddess who lives in the reeds," an old man from the front of her boat said.

Catherine smiled sympathetically, shading her eyes from the rising sun. She could see Josh in the boat ahead of her. With his head and shoulders outlined against the sky, he might have been the sun god himself.

But he wasn't a god; she knew that. He was a man and he wanted her as much as she wanted him. But he had more restraint than she did. He'd fallen asleep before she'd even finished undressing, while she'd lain awake for hours, thinking about him. She reminded herself of her vow to keep everything on a business basis. It was clear he hadn't forgotten, and she was grateful for that. Grateful, but also a little disappointed.

In the middle of the lake the men gave her a pole and showed her where to drop her line. In a few minutes she had a trout, and then another and another. By midmorning they were dragging a bucket of large fish behind the boat. Voices echoed across the lake as the men in her canoe shouted to the men in his canoe. One of the young men in her boat confided that when they got their motorboat they would be able to use gill nets. The cannery would buy all they could catch and they would be rich. She asked what they did with the extra fish they caught now. He told her the women took them to town to barter for salt and flour and supplies.

The boats met for lunch on a small island where the men built a fire and cooked fish. Josh took Catherine aside and they sat on the shore, looking out at the treeless hills that surrounded the lake, eating crisp filets fried over the open fire.

"So far so good," he said. "The lake seems to be full of trout. I caught six myself. But I didn't see much else. I hear the

trout did away with the smaller fish that were here origi-
nally.''

She nodded. There was something about that that disturbed her.

"They really know what they're doing," he continued en-
thusiastically. "And I agree that riding in a balsa boat is like
riding a bucking bronco. I thought you were going to fall
overboard at first." He watched the wind blow her hair into a
tangle of curls and felt the same stab of fear again as he had
when he thought her boat was capsizing.

"I thought so, too. But now I'm kind of used to it."

"The motorboats will be faster and they'll have better control," he said, noticing the way the wind whipped the color
into her cheeks.

An uneasy feeling nagged at the corner of her mind. "What
about the sleeping goddess?" she asked. "How will she feel
when the motorboats come ripping through here?"

He studied her face, counting the freckles the sun had dusted
across her nose. "Who?" he asked at last.

"She lives in the reeds at the bottom of the lake. That's why
we paddled gently."

The full intensity of her liquid dark eyes caught him, and he
felt his mind reeling. "Are you making this up?"

"No, you can ask the old man in my boat." Frowning
slightly, she laid her hand on his. "I like these people. I want
them to get their boats and their gill nets, but . . . but . . ."

"But you think the sleeping goddess or the sun god might
object?"

She shook her head. "I'm serious. I've heard stories of what
happened in Alaska to the salmon. The canneries came in and
subsidized the fishermen. They abandoned their trawlers and
went for floating factories. When the waters were fished out,
the Department of Fish and Game had to shorten the season.
One year it was twenty-four hours. Can you imagine how that
would affect their lives?"

"Catherine," he said, leaning forward. "This is Lake Cordillera. Those were salmon. These are fresh-water trout."

"I know," she said quickly. "But look how balanced their
lives are, these people. They have a surplus of fish, yes, but
they trade them for what they need. They live in harmony with

nature, like we do in Palomar. They have plenty to eat, like we do in the village. But their men don't go off for weeks at a time like the men in Palomar do."

He stood slowly and looked out across the choppy water. "Are you telling me you don't think they should get the loan?"

"No, of course not. It's your decision."

He shook his head. "It's Duran's decision. We're here to gather facts and give him our opinion."

She stood and brushed the crumbs off her pants. "Sometimes the price of a loan is too high."

The men pushed the balsas back into the water for the return trip. Catherine rolled her pants up and waded into the water. In the boat she trailed her hand in the water as the paddles dipped silently in and out. She felt a sinking sensation in her heart. She didn't envy Duran if he decided to turn them down. Maybe he would or maybe he'd follow his inclination and give it to them.

She looked over her shoulder across the blue-green water at Josh in the boat behind her. Even from that distance she could see his brow was furrowed and he was thinking it over. Maybe the villagers would be able to maintain a balance between efficient fishing and overfishing even with motorboats. But she was worried. Was this what it was like to take an uncomfortable, unpopular stand? Is this what bankers did every day?

Back on the island the children were just leaving the schoolhouse. Miguel's son waved to them and shyly invited them to come with him to visit his uncle, who was a boat builder. The boy was clutching the toy boat he had been working on the night before.

Josh smiled and Catherine said they'd be happy to meet the boat builder. "I think I know what your recommendation will be," Josh said as they followed the boy along the path to his uncle's.

Feeling a twinge of guilt, she answered, "Don't listen to me. I don't know anything about making loans or fishing for that matter. Forget what I said."

"I can't. What's happened to the woman who made up her mind before she even got here?" He took her hand and they walked side by side down the path lined with reeds.

"She's here. But she's confused. I want what's best for the people and what's best for you . . ."

"But you're not sure what that is and neither am I," he confessed.

She glanced up at him. "If this is what it's like to be a banker, then I feel sorry for you."

He pulled her close, his hip hard and solid against hers. "Don't. Sometimes banking has unexpected rewards. Sometimes someone comes to my office by mistake."

"Like me?" she asked. "That was no mistake."

"And asks for something impossible," he continued.

"Like a loan to buy a truck?"

"And I say no."

"But you feel bad about it."

He nodded and smoothed her hair with his hand.

"So you change your mind." She turned and pressed her palms against his. "Josh, I don't want to let you down."

The emotion in her voice surprised him. He motioned the boy to go on ahead and linked his arms loosely around her waist. "You're not going to let me down. What's happened to you? I'll never forget your telling me all you wanted was some small change and you asked me what I had to lose."

"That was before I knew you, before I realized what you had to lose. Before I realized how much your job means to you."

"No more than yours means to you." He slid his hands up her arms until he held her by her shoulders.

Her braid had come undone and the loose tendrils framed her face and softened her earnest expression. "This is just one of my jobs. The farm in Palomar is just one of the many farms I'm going to work and the Mamara are just one tribe of Indians I'm going to help. It's not the same for you."

He watched, fascinated, while her cheeks turned pink as she grew more animated.

"You're moving up and I'm moving sideways," she explained. The sun shone on her dark hair as the smell of reeds drying in the sun at the boat builder's house wafted their way. The boy had long ago disappeared down the path, and they were alone, hidden from view by the tall grasses.

"Then how do you think our paths crossed?" he asked, tucking a dark wisp of hair behind her ear.

"I don't know," she whispered. "But I'm glad they did."

He leaned forward and captured her face between his hands. He felt the warmth of her face, watched her take his hand in hers and kiss his broad palm. The touch of her lips made him want to wrap her in his arms and disappear behind the reeds to the soft grass by the shore. The thought of Catherine and him lying in the warm afternoon sun made the heat rise up the back of his neck.

Above the whisper of the wind in the reeds came the sound of a man wielding a machete in the clearing beyond, reminding Josh of his obligations to the fishermen of the village, to Duran and to the bank. This was a business trip. There were decisions to be made and people to see. The uncle, for one. Without speaking Josh took Catherine's hand and they walked toward the house of the boat builder. The uncle was there, his machete on the ground. His sun-browned face broke into a smile at the sight of the visitors. Proudly he showed them how he formed the sides and then the heart of the boat with the materials at hand.

Then he turned his attention to the small toy boat his nephew had brought and they all walked down to the water to try it out. Catherine knelt on the wooden pier to watch the boat float in the clear, shallow water. It was as carefully made as the ones they had ridden in that morning.

She caught Josh's eye and she wondered if he feared what she did. That if the village had motorboats, this craft might be lost. Not just this craft, but a whole way of life. Slowly they made their way back to Miguel's house where his wife was spinning wool from their llama into yarn.

"My mother spun her own yarn," Catherine said. "I never had a store-bought sweater until I grew up. She taught me to spin, too." She nodded to Miguel's wife, and she and Josh wandered down to the shore where the boats were drying in the sun.

"How can you say they left you nothing?" Josh asked, sitting on the beach, looking at her thoughtfully. "Besides your memories, they gave you skills, like weaving and cooking and plowing."

She squinted at the choppy waves with the sun dancing on them. "Everything but bargaining," she acknowledged with a half smile. "What are we going to report back to the bank?" She sat next to him and hugged her knees to her chest.

"That the coming of the cannery will bring the motorboats to this lake whether we like it or not."

"It's called progress," she mused, "and I guess it's inevitable."

"If this village doesn't have them, they won't be able to compete," he said. "We can't let that happen."

She shook her head, relieved that they didn't have to disappoint these people she had come to admire and respect. He helped her to her feet, and silently they walked back to the schoolhouse.

On the path he imagined how the stillness of the lake would one day be broken by the roar of the boats, and it wasn't a pleasant thought. So for now he relished the silence and the sight of Catherine just ahead of him, her dark hair caressing her shoulders. Even more than the silence he relished this time alone with her. A time when they reached a decision that satisfied them both. A time of unexpected harmony.

Inside the schoolhouse the desks were closed for the day and the windows shuttered. They changed clothes for the farewell party the villagers were giving for them.

"This has been an experience for me," Catherine said, smoothing the skirt of her pale blue cotton dress, "standing in a banker's shoes for a few days. It's given me a new appreciation of your profession."

"My profession? What about me?" he asked, crossing the room and laying the back of his hand against her windburned cheek.

She looked up to catch a flash of desire burning in his eyes. "I've always appreciated you," she said quickly, feeling her heartbeat quicken. Appreciate. It was a good safe word. Now if only he'd leave it at that. But he didn't. He tilted her chin with his hand, and she closed her eyes and struggled with the feelings she'd tried to suppress. When had appreciation turned to admiration and admiration turned to something else? Something dangerously close to love.

Was it the night he'd slept on her shoulder in the taxi? Or was it the day he told her about the silver mine? Maybe it was the night she'd cooked dinner for him and he'd shared his dreams with her. If only he'd let her help him make them come true. But he was afraid. Afraid to try. Afraid to fall. She knew something about that. The thought of the farm in California, the cold, stern face of a banker, the fields baking in the sun, brought a cold chill of fear to her heart. Yes, she understood that kind of fear. As long as she stayed here, as long as things went well on the land, she could keep it at bay.

She looked up at his face in half shadow under the swinging light bulb above them, unable to read his expression. "It must be time for the party," she suggested, grateful for the distraction, for any reason not to stay in this room, to prolong the moment when they had to go to bed next to each other on the straw mattresses.

Miguel's house was filled with music and laughter and food. The women in their bright skirts and their dark braids smiled shyly and greeted them warmly. They pressed cups of tea into their hands and led them to the best seats to watch the entertainment.

There was music and dancing. Catherine found herself clapping and swaying to the music, forgetting everything but the warmth and friendship of these people she scarcely knew and the man next to her who she felt she'd known all her life. Before they left they got directions for the Island of the Sun so they could go on their own at sunrise to experience for themselves the legend of the sun god.

They walked arm in arm to the schoolhouse. Without saying anything Catherine changed into her nightshirt in the small bathroom. When she came out, Josh was standing by the door, still wearing his blue jeans and plaid shirt with the sleeves up above the elbows.

She sat cross-legged on her mattress and looked up inquiringly. He cleared his throat. "I'm going out for a walk," he said hoarsely.

"A walk, now? Why?" she asked.

"You must know why." He reached for the doorknob. "I can't keep my eyes off you and I'm having trouble keeping my hands off you. I can't sleep next to you and I can't sleep when

I'm not next to you." He shook his head. "This doesn't make any sense. So I'm going out for a walk. Maybe it will clear my head." He gave her a crooked smile. "Anyway, it's almost time to get up and go to the island."

She swallowed hard. "Josh?"

Framed in the doorway, he paused. "Yes?"

"I feel the same way. I want you, but I know I can't have you."

"Why not?" he asked in a strangled voice.

"Why not?" she asked. "You know why not. We're going in different directions, like two shooting stars that happened to collide. And before there's any damage we'll dust ourselves off and be gone on our way. I'll never forget what you did for me and for the village. You took a chance on us and got us the truck." She took a deep breath. "Now it's my turn to help you with your goal. Old Pedro has offered to take you to the mine. Isn't that wonderful?" She paused and watched his face darken as if a storm cloud had passed.

"That's not my goal. I thought you understood that. It's a dream, that's all. My goal is to become a vice president of the bank. To never have to worry about money again. Chasing after silver isn't part of my plans."

Shivering, Catherine pulled the handwoven blanket up around her shoulders. She had spoiled the evening by bringing up the subject of the mine. Maybe she'd spoiled the whole trip. She clamped her mouth shut so as not to say any more. So as not to suggest that dreams are just as important as goals. And that it was important to know the difference between them.

He stared at her for a long moment. "I need some fresh air. I'll see you in the morning."

After the door closed behind him, Catherine squeezed her eyes shut. How could he walk out on her now when she felt so close to him? When they shared so much? She told herself it was best that he had. What would she do if he were here on the mattress next to her, warm and vital and tempting her to forget what she'd said about going in different directions? But if it was for the best, why did she feel so awful?

Chapter Nine

Catherine thought she'd never sleep, but she must have because the next thing she knew she felt his hand on her shoulder.

"The Island of the Sun, remember?" he whispered.

Her eyes flew open and she swung her legs over the edge of the straw mattress. She gazed into his blue eyes, which contrasted with his tanned face. Running her hand through her tangled hair, she managed to smile in the semidarkness.

"I hope you remember how to paddle that boat," he said, returning her smile as if they'd never had that conversation last night.

She nodded reassuringly and pulled on her long pants and sweatshirt over her nightshirt. Silently, as the gulls swooped overhead, they walked across the reed-lined path once again. They pushed off in the balsa boat they'd borrowed from Miguel under stars that shone in the thin mountain air, much brighter than in La Luz, brighter even than in Catherine's backyard.

Seated single file, they quietly dipped their paddles in the water and headed out of the lagoon toward the Isla del Sol. She didn't ask him where he'd slept or if he'd slept. She wanted to forget about last night. And it was easy, as they paddled in perfect harmony, to believe their hearts and souls were also traveling on the same wavelength.

She couldn't see Josh, who was sitting behind her, but she imagined his muscles flexing as he pulled his paddle through the water. And she pictured his body bending forward and back in time with hers. When the moon set, it was a ball of gold in the dark sky. Catherine gasped at the sight and dragged her paddle for a moment.

"Beautiful, isn't it?" Josh said, his voice so close and so deep she could only nod in agreement.

She reached over her shoulder, and he took her hand and held it tightly for a moment. She felt tears prick her eyelids at the sheer beauty of the sky and sea. She would never forget they had shared this moment together. Then they turned the boat in the direction of the island.

In a half hour they reached their destination and climbed a steep slope to the first of the ancient terraces that rose like huge steps to the top of the island. In the darkness Catherine stumbled and slipped backward into Josh's arms. Leaning against a large rock, he held her while she caught her breath. She closed her eyes and let him support her, feeling the muscles in his chest through his jacket.

"Take it easy," he murmured in her ear.

"I don't want to miss it," she said breathlessly. "This is our only chance." She reached for the rocky ledge above her, and with a boost from Josh she pulled herself up. In a moment he was beside her. "Thanks for being there to catch me," she said.

"I'll always be there," he said, his warm breath on her cheek. And he hoisted her to the next level.

Always. Forever. Those were just words. If anything was forever, it was her farmland, as close to a sure thing as there was in this world, and yet it was gone forever.

Near the top of the slope the outline of a rectangular pile of stone stood against the sky, the remnants of the House of Inca. One doorway was left. Out of breath and caked with dirt, Josh pulled Catherine up to stand there. Framed in the doorway, their shoulders touching, they stood waiting silently.

Suddenly the sky in the southeast lightened and the sun burst forth in golden splendor just as it had for the Incas. Just as it had for centuries. Catherine breathed a sigh of pure delight. She looked at Josh, and he tightened his arm around her shoulders.

"So Old Pedro changed his mind," he said. "I wonder why."

Catherine stared straight ahead, watching the sun and the sky, not daring to believe that Josh, too, might change his mind. "He had a dream," she explained, "where the *padrón* told him not to be afraid anymore."

Josh shielded his eyes from the dazzling sun. "If I go, will you come along?"

"Of course."

Without another word they climbed down over rough stones from terrace to terrace until they reached the shore below and their boat. This time the sun and the wind were at their backs as they paddled to the village. The boat seemed to fly effortlessly over the waves.

The wind ferry took them to the mainland. They carried their bags to the train station, over the cobbled streets, still feeling the motion of the boat beneath their feet.

"When would we go to the mine?" she asked cautiously when they settled into the lounge car for the return to Castillo. She was afraid to ask, but more afraid not to.

"As soon as I can get away," he said.

The words came easily, but Catherine noticed creases in his forehead. She imagined that his decision to pursue his father's dream wasn't an easy one. She wondered how and when he had changed his mind. Maybe during the night when he went out for a walk.

Josh changed the subject, and it occurred to Catherine as they ate their lunch in the dining car that Josh could talk about other things besides banking, like farming or lost civilizations, and he was always interesting. She'd always assumed that bankers' wives must be bored out of their minds talking to their husbands about the prime rate and variable interest mortgages. But being married to Josh would never be boring.

She felt the color rise in her face. How could she even think such a thing? What would the people in Tranquility say if they knew what she was thinking? That she must be lonely or depressed or homesick. But she wasn't any of those.

But when they got off the train and drove back to the valley she felt something that bordered on loneliness. Maybe it began when she saw her small house sitting there in the rain, looking as sad and neglected as a person who'd been deserted. Maybe it was when she said goodbye to Josh and watched him drive away. That was when she faced the emptiness of the house and the void in the pit of her stomach.

She'd lived alone in this house for eighteen months and never felt it before. But she'd never spent every minute of two days with someone before. She made a fire in the cook stove and Jacinda, seeing the smoke from her chimney, came by to tell her it had been raining since she'd left. She put on her jacket and they went out to inspect the soggy fields. They unplugged drainage ditches, but it was too wet to plant. The tomato plants were sitting in pools of water.

For two days she watched the rain come down from inside her house, feeling more and more restless. The only reason she ventured out was to make arrangements with Old Pedro for the trip to the mine. When they settled on a date, she sent a message to Josh and he came by the market to tell her Tuesday was fine.

Catherine was ready at dawn. She had packed her boots and her down vest, her binoculars and her oldest jeans the night before. Then she had rolled up her sleeping bag and put it by the front door. Now she paced back and forth, wondering what else to take. She'd never been prospecting before, but she felt the excitement rise as she pressed her face against the rain-spattered window. Where was he? Would he never come?

At midmorning a Jeep with rain flaps and a spare fuel can on the back pulled up in front of her house. Josh got out and came to the front door. "All set?" he asked, his eyes gleaming with anticipation.

She nodded and her heart skipped a beat. Was it the idea of discovering a lost silver mine, or the thought of going there with Josh? Whatever it was there was electricity in the air, and she knew he felt it, too. She grinned idiotically, unable to contain her excitement. He smiled back and she peered over his shoulder. "Where's Pedro?"

"In the back. He wanted to bring his burro, but I told him we didn't need one. We have four-wheel drive."

"Where did you get it?" she asked, impressed by its rugged exterior.

"I borrowed it from a customer who has a ranch in Callajita."

He picked up her duffel bag and sleeping bag. She looked around the room. "I hope I haven't forgotten anything. I have warm clothes. I found someone to drive the women to market...."

Impatiently he beckoned to her, and she closed the door behind them. In the Jeep she stowed her basket in back next to Pedro. She said hello, but he only gave her a brief nod. She hoped he hadn't changed his mind. Still, he was there, and she felt a sudden surge of confidence that they would find the mine.

After they left the valley, the rain tapered off. An hour later Pedro leaned forward to speak to them.

"He says you should leave this monster behind and pick up some burros to carry the equipment," Catherine said.

"How long would it take by burro?" Josh inquired.

"Longer than the Jeep, but he knows they're surefooted."

"Tell him this monster will take us farther faster. Like this." Josh turned abruptly off the road and onto a rocky riverbed. Catherine braced her feet against the floor and Pedro's eyes widened in surprise. "That's four-wheel drive," he explained, heading toward a mahogany tree where he parked under its gigantic branches.

As they got out of the Jeep and stretched, dozens of brightly colored birds emerged from the branches of the tree and took flight above them. Catherine tilted her head back as they flew in a pattern against the morning sky.

Pedro exclaimed and Catherine translated. "He says it's a good sign. Parrots and toucans bring good luck."

"I hope he's right." Josh shielded his eyes from the sun. "We'll need all the luck we can get."

Catherine opened her basket and spread a cloth on the ground. "We also need lunch."

"You brought lunch? I thought we'd drive straight through. I want to get to Santa Cruz tonight and pick up our supplies."

"Josh. You've waited all these years. Can't we take a half hour for lunch?" She looked around at the mountains in the distance. "This is a beautiful spot for a picnic, and I made empanadas from Jacinda's recipe."

He stuffed his hands into his pockets. "Fine," he said. "Just so we get to the site tomorrow. If Pedro remembers where it is."

She handed him a meat-filled pastry. "And if he doesn't?"

He shrugged as if it didn't matter. "We'll come back and forget the whole thing."

Relieved at his change in attitude, she poured lemonade into metal cups for all of them. It didn't matter if he was acting casually for her benefit. She could see he was more relaxed lounging on the ground with an empanada in his hand than he'd been a few minutes ago.

As it turned out, they got to Santa Cruz with plenty of time to buy supplies—oil for their lantern, fuel for their camp stove and some food. Encouraged by their progress, Josh pressed on to the road to Tochabamba with night falling around them. He seemed driven by an inner force to get to the mine that night instead of the next day.

With her nose pressed to the window Catherine heard Josh ask Pedro if he remembered the route, but there was so little daylight that he said no. The road twisted upward, narrower and narrower until it was only one lane and dropped off steeply to one side. Catherine closed her eyes and pressed her lips together to keep from protesting.

Suddenly Josh swerved and stopped abruptly. Catherine's eyes flew open. In the dusk she made out the words on a wooden sign: Lookout Point. They were in a clearing shaped like a semicircle and rimmed with rocks to prevent vehicles from driving off into the valley below.

One glance at his white knuckles and clenched jaw told her he'd been almost as worried as she was and that they weren't going any farther that night. Slowly she got out of the Jeep.

Pedro followed cautiously. The older man obviously would have preferred his slower, safer burro ride.

"Great view," she said with all the enthusiasm she could muster. She tried to ignore the twinge of vertigo that hit her when she looked down at the white ribbon of road they'd just taken. "We've come a long way," she remarked.

"But we've still got a long way to go," he said with a worried frown.

Impulsively she wrapped her arms around him as if she could somehow ease his worries that way. "Maybe not that long," she murmured, her cheek against his soft flannel shirt. "Tomorrow, when it's light, things will look different. More familiar."

She felt the muscles in his chest relax as he leaned over and buried his face in her hair. "Did I tell you I'm glad you came with me?" he asked in a deep, muffled voice.

She looked up at him, her arms linked around his waist. "I'm glad, too. This is the adventure of a lifetime. Your adventure. Thanks for sharing it with me."

He gave her a quick, fierce kiss. He wanted to share everything with her. Adventures, disasters, whatever came. But she'd made it clear that wasn't what she wanted. She wanted to share her adventures with farmers in South America, helping them have better yields and better lives. As for him, he had to put his dream to rest, once and for all, so he could get on with his life. A life that didn't include Catherine Logan. Suddenly that prospect seemed so bleak that he kissed her again, harder and with more intensity as if he could change things that way.

Catherine stood very still, absorbing the pressure of his kiss, wanting it to go on forever. But she straightened and turned so that her back was to the steep drop-off. "Looks like a good campsite," she said, still breathless from the kiss.

"As long as no one else decides to camp here, too," he remarked with a smile. Her relentless good humor cheered him up, gave him hope.

"We haven't passed a single car for miles. I think we'll have the place to ourselves."

He looked around. "No place to attach a tarpaulin."

She shrugged. "We'll sleep under the stars."

Josh nodded. He opened the door to the Jeep and folded the front seats down so that Pedro could sleep inside. Catherine lifted her wicker basket from the rear, glad she'd brought plenty of food and wine, glad that the worry lines between Josh's eyebrows had disappeared.

They all sat cross-legged around the tablecloth. This time there were no trees, no birds, only the stars overhead and, if one looked, the lights of the houses in the valley twinkling below. Catherine didn't look. Instead she looked at Josh eating a sandwich of bread and cheese by starlight. He leaned back on one elbow and looked at her.

"Do you remember the Fourth of July?" he asked.

"We had hot dogs and champagne." She looked up at the stars.

"You wore a short skirt and a T-shirt," he recalled. "It was the first time I saw your legs."

She smiled in the dark. "You wore a blue shirt. It was the first time I saw you without a suit." It was the first time she'd thought of him as anything but a banker. Maybe it was the first time he'd thought of her as anything but a farmer. There was a long silence. With a friendly good-night Pedro retired to the Jeep.

"You missed the fireworks," he said. "I owe you a sparkler and some rockets. I owe you a whole night of fireworks."

Her hands shook as she folded the tablecloth and put it in the basket. In the stillness of the night his words hung in the air. He went to the Jeep, took out their sleeping bags and placed them on the ground next to each other. She pictured their bodies locked together under a starry sky, making fireworks together, but she knew she couldn't let that happen. Not tonight. Not any night.

She brushed her teeth behind the Jeep with mineral water. Then she removed her shoes and slid into her down bag. He was lying next to her with his arms crossed under his head. A shooting star sped across the sky.

"There you are. Natural fireworks," she said.

"That's not what I meant," he growled.

She sighed and turned her back to him. If she looked into his eyes, she'd be lost. She didn't want to hear him breathe or imagine his arms around her. This was a discovery trip, an expedition with no room for runaway emotions. No time for indulging in passions they'd later regret.

Despite the hard ground, despite the nearness of Josh, she slept. She slept so well that only the sun shining in her eyes and the smell of coffee woke her up. Surprised, she blinked her eyes and sat up, the sleeping bag at her waist. Josh smiled down at her from behind a cup of steaming coffee.

"Wait a minute. Where did you get that? I thought you couldn't cook."

He tilted his head in the direction of Pedro bent over the camp stove, stirring fried potatoes. "I can't, but Pedro can. Good thing. If we'd waited for you, we'd starve."

She got up and tied her sleeping bag into a tight roll. After breakfast they stood next to the Jeep. The deep crease was back between Josh's eyebrows.

"Would you ask Pedro," he said, "if anything looks familiar today." Pedro shook his head. Josh nodded curtly. "We'll go on a little farther."

Back in the Jeep Catherine closed her eyes so that she couldn't see the sharp drop-off to the right. Around the next bend Pedro leaned forward and squinted into the distant hills that undulated under a bright blue sky.

"The sleeping maiden," he said slowly in Spanish.

Josh met Pedro's eyes in the rearview mirror. "Is that where it is?" He'd never heard of the sleeping maiden. Still, it was possible.

"The mine is to the east." Pedro pointed to a barren, rocky mountain. "That's Tochabamba."

Josh slowed to a crawl as Catherine translated for him. "Fine. We know where it is. We just don't know how to get there."

Pedro put his hand on Josh's shoulder and spoke.

"He says you can get burros from the ranch ahead, then follow the trail to the mine."

Josh's eyes widened. "Is it possible that the ranch is still here after all these years?"

Another twenty miles up the road was an arrow pointing west. The sign had fallen onto its side, but the letters were still legible: Rancho del Cielo. They drove down a rutted road and followed tracks made by the wheels of a cart until a ramshackle house came into view. It looked deserted, but when they cut the engine, the silence of the mountain air was broken by the braying of burros and the clucking of chickens. Catherine gave Josh a look of surprise.

An old man came around the corner of the house more astonished to see them than they were to see him. Pedro tipped his hat. Catherine didn't know if they were acquainted or not, but Pedro was able to borrow three burros and buy more food for the journey. They filled their saddlebags and tied their sleeping bags onto the burros. Catherine rubbed her hands against her pants and looked inquiringly at Josh.

His eyes were on the distant mountains. "Are you sure' you're up to this? It must be a long walk. With Pedro on a burro we'll need the other two to carry the equipment."

She laced up her boots. "I wouldn't miss it for anything." It was true. She was willing to go farther than the Tochabamba Mines to share Josh's dream.

Pedro showed no emotion as he mounted his burro and led the way down the trail. Josh wished he could control his emotions, as well. He was afraid there would be nothing at the end of the trail. But he wanted desperately to find something, anything. He tried to empty his mind and enjoy the walk through the long valley, knowing there would be a steep climb ahead.

The sun shone down, warming his head and shoulders, easing the tension. Ahead of him he heard the clip-clop of the burros and he watched Catherine, admiring her hips swaying slightly in her loose-fitting pants. She wore a soft canvas hat that protected her head from the sun. She'd braided her hair that morning while he'd drunk his coffee, but soft tendrils had escaped and curled at the nape of her neck.

He imagined how soft her hair would feel wrapped around his fingers. He knew how her skin would taste if he kissed the back of her neck, like sage and sunshine, like all outdoors. He caught up with her where the trail widened and he fell into step.

"Are you getting tired?" he asked.

She shook her head. Tiny flecks of hazel lightened her eyes. "This is the best trip I've ever had. I feel as if we've come to another world. Everything's different here, the sun, the earth, everything." She gazed off at the wide alkali flats and the eroded mountains streaked with red in the distance, then turned back to him. "Even us," she said softly. "We're different, too."

He stopped and drew her to him, running his hand up her neck to caress the soft curls that escaped from her braid. "You're the same," he protested, "still beautiful, still desirable. I wouldn't be here without you. I wouldn't *want* to be here without you. I don't want to be anywhere without you," he said with a quick kiss before they continued along the trail.

This time he took the lead. Catherine ran her finger across her lips, feeling the warmth of his kiss still lingering. Later they stopped for lunch at the entrance to a steep canyon. Above them were names carved in the stone wall. Josh read the names and the dates, but his father's name wasn't there.

Catherine removed her boots slowly and stretched out her legs. Josh sat opposite her and took her feet into his lap. Starting a massage at her heel and working his way under the arch, he made her bones turn to liquid. She arched her back and let her head fall back.

"That feels so good," she moaned softly. "Where did you learn to do that?"

"I make it up as I go along," he confessed, his fingers unleashing a fire that would be out of control if she didn't stop it. Reluctantly she pulled away.

"I'm not sure I'll ever be able to get up again," she said in a shaky voice.

But when Pedro cooked an omelet on the stove, she managed to get to her feet and take her plate. She and Josh ate next to each other with their backs against the wall, feeling the sun-warmed stone through their shirts.

Pedro stood and scanned the canyon while Josh followed his eyes. Finally he spoke. "He says we'll be there by tonight," Catherine said, standing and tying her jacket around her waist. Her eyes glowed, and Josh worried that she was counting on finding silver. He could handle his own disappointment, but not hers, too.

Pedro tied the three burros together with a rope and they began to climb. On every slope they saw telltale signs of old workings, piles of stones marking a strike or a rusted tobacco tin. Narrow trails led off to remote areas, to God knew where.

Pedro stopped for a long moment and looked around. Josh's heart sank. It was clear to him they were lost. It was too late to go back. They'd have to find a place to stay along the trail and go back tomorrow. But Pedro kept going. And they followed. Followed him down a salt-encrusted draw and turned around. They watched him look up at the sky, either to get his bearings or to ask God for help. They weren't sure which. Josh's spirits dropped and his feet felt heavy.

He noticed that even Catherine's step had lost its spring. She wiped the perspiration off her brow with the sleeve of her shirt. "Does he know where he's going?" Josh asked from behind her.

"It's been forty years," she explained in a tired voice. "Things change. Landslides. Earthquakes." She reached for his hand. "Don't worry. If he says we'll be there tonight, we'll be there."

At dusk they were crisscrossing the side of a barren mountain, the burros' hooves sending loose stones down hundreds of feet. Catherine stopped and clung to a boulder. She kept her eyes fastened on Pedro. Her feet were numb, her breath short and her hands clammy. She couldn't move.

Josh came up behind her. "Are you all right?" he asked anxiously.

She didn't turn around. "As long as I don't look down." Her voice was taut with tension.

Carefully he stepped in front of her, took her hand and pulled her forward across the loose stones. "Just keep your eyes on me and don't let go. This is a hell of a place for a person with vertigo."

Her eyes latched onto his and didn't let go. The intensity of his gaze gave her the strength to follow him. She didn't allow herself to think of the canyon below. She thought of him, only of him and put herself, quite literally, into his hands. His grip was warm and strong, and he pulled her steadily as the switchbacks took them higher and higher.

Suddenly Pedro and the burros disappeared over the top of a ledge, and the only sound was the wind whistling through the canyon. Despite his hold on her hands, Catherine's step faltered and she squeezed her eyes shut for a moment.

"Look at me," he ordered, and she obeyed. His blue eyes reflected the sky above, and in his gaze she found the courage to go on. "It's only a few more feet. Pedro's already there," he assured her.

At the top she fell forward into his arms and he held her tightly. His shirt was cool and dry against her cheek. She was embarrassed by her vertigo, but he patted her on the back as if she'd just climbed Everest. She wound her arms around his neck and wished she could stay there forever. Forever. That word again.

She dropped her arms and slowly looked around. They were standing in an amphitheater ringed by rocky and barren mountains in air so clear that the Cordera Range, more than two hundred miles away, was a blue-purple mass. In between lay green fields and willows. To the west was the sun setting on the Esquinas River.

She was so intent on the view that she almost missed the rubble at their feet. Huge stones and rocks lay in heaps as if a giant had tossed them about. Pedro was right. The God of Thunder had surely been there.

"Where's Pedro?" she asked, and they looked around. Suddenly he appeared from an opening in the side of the mountain, his small body dwarfed by the rock that had blocked him from sight. A smear of mud covered his forehead.

"The shaft has opened again," he said flatly, but his eyes betrayed his emotion. "Somewhere inside are the bodies of the miners, my friends." He shook his head and tears filled his eyes.

Josh put his hand on the old man's shoulder, able to understand his sense of loss and realizing what the words meant. "We won't stay long," he promised. "Just long enough to take samples and bring them home."

From a saddlebag Josh dug out his lantern. He knelt on the ground and carefully filled it with gas, pumped it up and lit the mantle. In the dusk it cast a dim light on the expectant faces of Catherine and Pedro. He wanted to tell them now what he knew in his heart. There was no silver there. There were only lost dreams and lives. Failure and disappointment. But he couldn't say it. They'd have to see for themselves.

"Let's go," he said, walking to the entrance.

"Now?" Catherine looked around at the vast emptiness, the cold rocks and the darkening sky. Pedro shook his head and backed away. Josh didn't see him.

He was only dimly aware of the apprehension in Catherine's voice. His heart was pounding, his pulse racing. Was this the feeling that drove men to leave their families and sail for California in 1849? Was this what made his father leave his family to travel the four corners of the globe? Was this what they called gold fever?

"Now," he said, and she followed him to the opening of the tunnel. Suddenly it was dark and cold. She shivered and he grabbed her hand. The lantern cast its beam down a narrow tunnel, caked with black mud. The clammy walls seemed to close in on them, and the mud oozed at their feet.

"If the mine caved in once, couldn't it happen again?" she asked, tightening her grip on his hand. A spider scuttled across the toe of her boot while she watched in fascinated horror. When it disappeared from view, she bent down to pick up a chunk of gray rock with a streak of red running through it.

"Do you want to wait outside?" he asked.

"No," she assured him, slipping the rock into her pocket. "I've already found something. Maybe it's valuable. Who knows?"

"The avalanche seems to have been much farther back." He shone the lantern on the slats of wood that braced the walls and the ceiling. "I think we're safe here." He scraped a blob of mud from the wall and held it in his hand.

"What is it?" she asked, her pulse quickening.

"Probably just mud, but we'll take it and have it analyzed."

"It doesn't look like silver."

"Silver weathers and oxidizes. It's hard to identify by sight." In his mind he saw the gleam and felt the smooth surface of the precious metal, and he knew deep down there wasn't any in this mud. "Tomorrow we'll go farther, as far as we can. If it's there, we'll find it. But silver is tricky. Sometimes it's found with lead or zinc."

Surprised by his knowledge of mining, she followed him out into the fresh night air. Inhaling deeply, she asked, "How do you know all this? From your father?"

He shook his head. "I've been doing some reading."

The sight of Pedro roasting a chicken over the open fire made her realize how hungry and tired she was. Her knees buckled under her, and Josh caught her under the arms.

"Whoa," he said, lowering her gently next to the fire. "Are you okay?"

"I'm fine," she told him, holding her hands out to warm them by the hot coals. He knelt behind her and massaged the tired muscles in her neck until her head fell forward and a sigh escaped her lips. "Still making it up as you go along?" she murmured.

Instead of answering, he kissed the back of her neck while his hands continued to work their magic on her shoulders. If there was heaven on earth, it would feel like this, she thought. Gradually his palms moved to the small of her back, and just when she thought she couldn't stand another moment of this exquisite pleasure, Pedro coughed loudly to get their attention. Dinner was ready.

They ate around the fire, tearing the chicken off the bones with their fingers. When they finished, Pedro placed his bedroll as far from the entrance to the mine as possible, while Catherine and Josh put theirs next to the fire.

She pulled her sleeping bag up to her chin, a thousand questions on her mind. She watched the firelight play on Josh's face, turning his eyes into fathomless holes, his jaw to chiseled rock.

"What if there isn't any silver?" she asked at last. "What will you do?"

"Walk away from it," he said. "What else can I do?" He lay back and looked at the sky. "I didn't come for the silver, not really. It would just be a bonus." He didn't say what he had come for, but she knew. He had come to find himself. To find the dreamer within himself and make room for that part of himself in his life. If he couldn't do that, there wouldn't be room for her, either.

If Josh had come to find himself, what had she come to find? Had she come to find out what kind of a man he was? If so, the trip was a success. He was strong, but not macho. He was tender, but not weak. He could make her laugh and make her cry, too. He could make her want him in a way that made her feel worse than she'd ever felt before. But he could make her feel happier than she ever thought possible. What if it doesn't work out? she asked herself. And she knew the answer. Walk away from it, she told herself. What else could she do?

She brought her arm out of her sleeping bag and reached for Josh. He rolled over and faced her. Taking her hand in his, he pulled her close to him and put his arms around her sleeping bag. She sighed, buried her head on his shoulder and felt the warmth of his body through the thick padding of her sleeping bag until she fell asleep.

The air was cool in the morning. They stood around the fire in their down vests, drinking coffee, their eyes drawn involuntarily to the entrance to the mine. Josh set his cup down and rubbed his hands together. He studied Catherine's face, noticing the lines etched between her eyebrows. Cupping her chin in his hand, he smiled reassuringly.

"Don't worry," he said. "I don't need the silver. Neither does Pedro. Whatever happens our lives will go on."

She nodded automatically, but he didn't think he'd convinced her. Maybe he hadn't convinced himself yet. It was true he didn't need the silver. But he needed something else. What it was he didn't know. He wouldn't know until he found it.

"Are you ready?" he asked, a shovel in one hand, the lantern in the other, and a pouch attached to his belt for samples.

Catherine grabbed the pickax, and with Pedro watching from a safe distance, they entered the long tunnel to the mine again. She shone her flashlight on the rocks, and a scorpion crawled out and ran from them. She clamped her lips together to keep from screaming. Particles from the ceiling showered them as they walked. Catherine shook her head and captured some in her hand.

When she spoke, her voice was a whisper. "Silver dust?"

Dubiously he looked at her palm. "Put it in the bag," he instructed. When they reached the end of the tunnel, Josh leaned against the loose dirt wall. Looking down where his lantern cast its light, he saw an old rusty hand drill and next to it two pole picks.

He set his lantern down and knelt in the dirt. Bracing his hand on the ground, he felt something solid under the dirt. "Catherine, over here. Shine your light this way." He dug into the soft dirt with his fingers. His heart pounded with excitement. Was this what treasure hunting was all about, this feeling that the world had stopped spinning and everyone was holding their breath waiting...? After digging for a moment, he held up a soft, worn leather case in the palm of his hand.

Catherine shone her light on it. "What is it?" she asked in a hushed voice.

He held the case up and pressed his fingers over the letters. When he tilted the case, a heavy object slid into his hand. "My father's magnifying glass," he said in a hollow voice.

He handed it to her and dug deeper into the soil before he found a compass, its cover cracked, its needle swinging wildly from north to south. "And his compass." He knelt for so long studying it that the lantern began to dim.

"Josh." Catherine's voice sounded worried. "Let's take the things out and get some air."

He stood stiffly and put the objects safely in his pocket. With the picks and the drill under their arms, they made their way back to the entrance. Squinting in the bright sunlight, Josh felt as dazed and shaken as if he'd been caught in the avalanche of forty years ago. When his eyes grew accustomed to the light, he sat on a rock and took the magnifying glass out of his pocket.

Pedro approached cautiously, relieved to see them again. Josh held out the magnifying glass for him to see.

"My father's," he said in Spanish, and Pedro's eyes grew round in his narrow face.

"*El padrón,*" he said. "Your father was the *padrón.*" Then he turned and went back to the mine, keeping watch for his old friends once more.

Catherine traced the initials JB on the leather.

"James Bentley," Josh said. "I knew he'd lost it. He had others, but they weren't the same. When he lost these things, he lost the silver mine, too. He thought there would be other mines, other ways to make a fortune, but you know what happened. He died broke." He turned it over in his hand. "Well, we found the glass, but not the silver." Disappointment settled over him like a dark cloud.

Catherine knelt at his side. She leaned forward, her dark eyes intense. "You said you didn't need the silver. You said it didn't matter."

"It doesn't matter, not to me. But it mattered to him. I wanted to find it for him. So he could be a success. At last." Josh stuffed the magnifying glass back into his pocket and stared across to the mountains beyond the valley without seeing them. "I didn't realize how much I wanted it." Bitterness, hurt and disappointment filled his throat and choked off his words. Catherine rose and stood at his side.

"Can you believe my father spent his life thinking about this place?" he asked her, looking around at the barren outcroppings. "What a waste." He shook his head. "That's the part that gets me. That a man could waste his life looking for lost treasure."

Catherine's heart ached, for Josh, for his father and for herself. For Josh, finding the treasure would have meant finding himself. For herself it would have meant finding a man who allowed himself to have both dreams and goals. Her eyes filled with tears.

"There are worse things," she said with a catch in her throat. The sun was straight overhead, but she shivered.

He shoved his hand into his pocket and fingered the magnifying glass, then looked at her inquisitively.

She struggled to find the right words. "I mean, at least he followed his dream. He didn't spend his life working in an office, wondering what it would be like—"

"You can say that again. He never had a steady job in his life."

"I understand that. But he never had second thoughts. He knew what he wanted to do and he did it."

"Oh, Catherine," he said in exasperation. "You didn't know him."

"Did you?"

"Of course I did. I'm the one who listened to his stories. He almost made a believer out of me. He was Paul Bunyon and Peter Pan and Daniel Boone. The man who never gave up. The man who never grew up. I'll never forgive him. But I'll never forget him, either," he added under his breath. Then Josh lifted his arms and stretched them toward the sky. "Okay, Dad, I'm here," he shouted. "Where's the treasure?"

The word echoed off the purple mountains and mocked him. Treasure...treasure...treasure.

Catherine turned and met Josh's gaze. "Where should I look?" he called again, and the voice came back. Look... look...look.

Josh looked down at the compass in his hand. The needle swung around and pointed to Catherine and to the mine entrance behind her. He felt his heart speed up. He was on the brink of a discovery. Maybe even on the threshold of finding the answer. Just look, his father's voice seemed to say. Look around you. The gap that led to the mine was there ahead of him. Tantalizing him with its promise of riches. Empty promise. Empty mine.

He stared into the black depths of the cavern. The compass needle swung again and pointed back to himself. And suddenly he understood. "You're right," he said, sliding the compass into his pocket so he could put her hands on his hips. "I didn't know him. I didn't know why he left me the shares to the mine. Not until now."

"I don't understand. There was nothing in there but his tools. The shares are still worthless."

"That's what I thought, but I was wrong. I said he didn't leave me anything, but he did." Puzzled, Catherine looked into his eyes. He drew her to him and savored the warmth of her body after the cold, damp air of the mine. "I think he left me the mine so I could see for myself what it's like to be on the brink of the unknown," he said slowly, "to make a discovery of my own."

"What did you discover?" she asked.

"I discovered that I'm part dreamer like my father. That I'm drawn to the unknown just as he was. I wasn't supposed to come to Aruaca. I was scheduled to go to Panama, and then Colombia, but I turned them down and put my career in jeopardy, not knowing what would happen, hoping something here would open up. This job turned up, I turned up and you turned up, all at the same time."

"So your father was a success, after all. He got you here."

"He got us both here."

"And now you know what he wanted you to know. How do you feel?"

His answer was to lift her in the thin mountain air and spin her around. Her hair fell around her face in a cloud of waves. Her cheeks reddened and she laughed out loud. It was joy. It was relief. It was the most beautiful sound he'd ever heard. When he set her down, he smiled.

"How do I feel? I feel good for myself, but sorry for my father. I wish he could see me now."

Catherine looked off at the clouds massing over the mountains in the distance. "Maybe he can. Maybe he knows. Maybe that was his voice you heard."

"That was an echo," he said, but there was a hint of doubt in his voice that made her smile. He traced the outline of her upturned lips with his finger. "All right, maybe it was his voice. Maybe he knows I'm here. And he knows you're here with me. Maybe he planned the whole thing. Today I believe anything's possible."

"Like your promotion?"

"Yes. No. I wasn't thinking about that. In fact, I haven't thought about it for days, maybe weeks. It doesn't seem so important anymore. What's more important is what I found here. I feel like I found the piece to a puzzle that I didn't even know was missing. Does that make sense to you?"

She wiped her dusty hands on her pants. "I think so. What's next?" Her words hung in the still mountain air. The silence was broken only by the buzzing of bees near some wildflowers growing in a crack in the rocks.

A jolt of elation hit him. A weight had been lifted from his shoulders, freeing him to do whatever he wanted. To be whatever he wanted to be. He was no longer afraid of poverty or insecurity. The only thing he was afraid of was losing Catherine.

In answer to her question he kissed her, tenderly at first, then passionately. He pulled away to look into her face. "I feel like anything's possible . . . you . . . me . . . anything."

"Yes," she agreed breathlessly, "but . . ."

Whatever it was he didn't want to hear it. He didn't want to hear her say she didn't love him or that there was no future for them because of her five-year plan, or her determination not to return to the States. Not now. Now when they were on top of the world, the only two people in the world. So he kissed her again to seal her lips.

She lifted her arms and hugged him to her, returning his kiss, deepening and lengthening it until they staggered backward toward the mine together, their shoes scraping across the stones and gravel. He caught her around the waist and stared into her eyes, looking for a sign that she believed in them, in their future.

Catherine felt as if her body was on fire. It wasn't fair of him to ask her what she thought when she couldn't think at all. She could only feel, and what she felt was that whether it was his father or fate, something had brought them together to the top of this mountain. And she wouldn't, she couldn't, cast a shadow over his dreams.

"It . . . it's been quite a day," she stammered, avoiding his gaze, knowing there were questions there she couldn't answer. She felt a rumble of laughter in his chest at her understatement.

"And it's not over yet," he said, looking down at her. "I want to go back inside. I want a sample of every kind of rock there is. I don't know why, but I do."

She picked up the shovel and leaned on it to support her shaky knees. "Okay."

Together, with Pedro watching and helping when he could, they made many trips in and out of the mine, carrying small samples. Catherine was at Josh's side, sharing the elation of discovery. She wondered what would happen when they got back to sea level. Would this euphoria disappear when he found the rocks were worthless and things didn't seem so simple? Anything was possible for them. But probable? No. He said he hadn't thought about his promotion, but he hadn't said he didn't want it. He was still going back to become a vice president someday.

They spent their last night at the mine, stretched out next to the fire. He tucked her body next to his to protect her from the cool night air and buried his face in the fragrance of her dark hair. He wanted to tell her how he felt now, so she could get used to the idea that he loved her. But he was just getting used to it himself and he wondered if she was ready to hear it yet. Her steady breathing told him she was already asleep, so he lay awake and watched the embers of the fire, his mind spinning with hopes, dreams and plans.

After they packed their saddlebags the next day, they headed down the mountain. Josh helped Catherine down the steep, rocky grade just as he'd helped her up. She kept her eyes fastened on his, her hands tightly gripping his. He willed her his strength and her feet found the path. He almost told her then, as they paused to get their bearings, the hot sun on their shoulders, the sound of the burros' hooves ahead of them, what he'd decided to do about her and about them, but he didn't.

He walked behind her across the valley, his eyes on the curve of her hips, and resolved not to say anything to spoil the magic of this trip. Walking in his father's footsteps, he thought about success. Success could be measured in other ways besides money. His father knew that. Catherine knew it, too. But he was just learning.

At the ranch they paid for the use of the burros, unpacked, thanked the old man and climbed into their Jeep for the long ride back to Palomar. It was still raining in their valley when they arrived the next evening. The skies were leaden and the ground was saturated. After leaving Pedro at his tin shop, Josh took Catherine to her house. When he unloaded her things, he found the rock she'd collected on the front seat.

"Don't forget your souvenir."

She ran her fingers over the vein of dark red that ran through the dull gray. "Have it analyzed with the other samples. Maybe I've got myself a ruby."

He smiled at the thought. "I'll do that. As soon as I get the results of the tests, I'll let you know." They took shelter from the rain on her front porch. "I have to get the Jeep back tonight, but I want to see you. We have to talk." Instead of talking, Josh bent down to kiss her lips, long and hard. He didn't want to leave. There was a nagging fear in the back of his mind that things would never be this good, this perfect again. He was afraid that if he left now something might come between them.

"I'll come by your stall tomorrow," he promised. He ran his hands down her arms and held her tightly. The dust from her shirt mingled with his. He kissed a smudge on her nose. A feeling of certainty replaced his doubts. Certainty that they belonged together, on a farm, or in a bank, along a trail or in a wobbly canoe.

Wherever she was, that was where he wanted to be. If he didn't feel so sure, he never would have left her on the steps, tired, dirty and disheveled. But it was only temporary. He'd bring the Jeep back, take a shower, leave the rocks to be analyzed and then tell Catherine what she already knew deep down in her subconscious: that their love was strong enough to overcome any obstacle. He kissed her long and slowly and left her standing on the steps looking dazed.

Chapter Ten

No sooner had Josh's car disappeared around the bend in the road than Jacinda appeared at Catherine's door, a waterproof poncho covering her small figure. Without wasting time with a greeting she pulled a basket of tomatoes from under her poncho and held it up for Catherine to see.

Catherine frowned at the white spots of mildew that dusted the tops of the tomatoes. "Oh, no," she murmured.

"Tomatoes need sun. Not much, but some," Jacinda said. "We cannot take these to sell."

"What about the potatoes or the melons?"

Jacinda shook her head. "Rotting in the fields."

A sick feeling hit Catherine with the force of a tractor. Mechanically she removed her jacket and boots and put water on the stove to boil for tea. Then she turned to Jacinda.

"What will we do?" the old woman asked, taking a seat at the kitchen table.

Catherine rubbed her hands together. "Wait," she said. "And while we have time on our hands, we'll knit for Magdalena's baby. Tell the women to come by this afternoon for a sewing bee."

Jacinda's narrow shoulders relaxed, and she smiled at Catherine. "I knew you would have the answer."

After Catherine poured the tea, Jacinda leaned forward across the table. "But what about the bank? We have not been there for many days. What will Mr. Bentley say when we do not appear with the payment?"

Catherine looked at the calendar on the wall. There was a large red circle around the seventeenth. "We have a few more days to worry about that. We'll think of something," she said with all the confidence she could manage. "Maybe the rain will stop by then."

Every day they crocheted blankets for the baby or knitted socks for the men in the mines, and still the rain came down. Restless, Catherine put her needles aside and went to the front window. It was so ironic that she almost laughed. Too much rain in Aruaca and too little in California. She finally wrote a letter to the bank to explain their problem, but the mailman's truck got stuck in the mud outside of town and no messages went in or out of Palomar for days. Josh must be wondering why they didn't show up at the stall or come by with the payment. But surely he would suspect it was because of the weather.

When the mailman finally dug his truck out, he brought a letter for Catherine. The women were in her kitchen, the sound of their voices blending with the click of the knitting needles. She saw the name of the bank in bold black letters in the corner of the envelope. Before she opened it she took a deep breath. When she scanned the print, certain words and phrases leaped out at her. They were "final notice," "vitally important," "further action" and "past due." The letter was signed by someone she'd never heard of. Catherine stood in the doorway of the kitchen, feeling the blood drain from her face.

Jacinda jumped up from the table and took Catherine's hands in hers. The letter fell to the floor. "Is it bad news from home?" she asked with a concerned frown on her wrinkled face.

Catherine steadied herself with one hand on the back of a chair. "No, not from home." She sat down with the women and explained what the letter meant. They argued that Josh

wouldn't do this, that they should talk with him, but in the end
they agreed that Catherine should take the truck back. They
tried to be strong, but their disappointment was obvious.
Catherine couldn't stand the look of sorrow on their faces any
longer. She turned and ran upstairs to change her clothes. As
she pulled off her long skirt and exchanged it for trim navy
blue pants and a matching jacket, she seethed with anger.

She knew the meaning of "further action." It was a euphe-
mism for "repossession." She could understand that. She
could understand their concern. But this form letter was so
impersonal. Did Josh know about it? Was it his idea? He knew
and she knew that she'd promised to bring the truck back if the
worst happened and they couldn't make their payments. Well,
the worst had happened and she'd bring the truck back to
where she'd gotten it in the lot behind the bank. Then she'd
ride up to his office and put the keys on his desk. If the bank
wanted to repossess the truck, she'd make it easy for them. She
said goodbye to the women, stuffed the letter into the pocket
of her jacket and drove out onto the highway.

It felt good to be behind the wheel again. It felt good to be
taking action, instead of sitting in the kitchen and watching the
rain come down. She'd had too many days to sit and think and
worry. But as she climbed up out of the valley, the rain increased until she could only see a few feet in front of her. It
didn't feel good to be behind the wheel anymore. She wished
herself back inside the kitchen, dry and safe.

The truck's tires slammed into rain-filled potholes, sending
sheets of muddy water up over the hood and onto the windshield. She gripped the steering wheel so tightly that her
knuckles were white. She veered to avoid a mud slide, sending
her to the edge of the road. The asphalt crumbled. She felt the
front left tire lose its support and roll over the edge.

She opened her mouth to scream, but no sound came out.
Trees rushed by and her head hit the roof with a thud. The
biggest tree she'd ever seen loomed in front of her and stopped
her wild, sickening ride with a jolt that crushed the front of the
truck. A pain shot through her chest as if she'd been speared,
and then everything went black.

Her last conscious thought was of Josh. His face floated in front of her and she heard his voice. "It's going to be okay," he said. "Everything's all right." But as the darkness pressed in on her, she knew that everything wasn't okay. And nothing was all right.

Josh stood at the corner of the cobblestone streets again at dawn as he'd done every day since he'd been back, watching the trucks rumble by. It was 7:00 a.m. and they weren't here. Again. Was it the truck or the rain, or had something else happened? He couldn't wait another day. He had to know.

He took a taxi to the bank and told his secretary he'd be out for a few hours. Then he headed his car out of town toward Palomar. The rain began about an hour after he left the city, light but steady. He didn't slow down. He looked at the sky, a sick, worried feeling nagging at his subconscious.

An hour later he saw the black tire marks veering off the road, and he screeched to a stop on the other side of the mud slide. In seconds he was standing at the edge of the asphalt where the road had crumbled away, his heart pounding, his hands shaking.

Bracing his feet on the steep slope, he saw the tracks leading down into the forest. Sliding, slipping, falling, he followed the tracks, skewed at impossible angles. He might have shouted her name if he'd had any air in his lungs, but he didn't. Finally, when he was halfway down the gulch, he saw the truck wedged into a huge fir.

She was slumped over the wheel, a huge bump on her forehead, a cut under her eye. He pried open the door and found his voice.

"Catherine." Her name was ripped from his throat.

She shuddered and he felt like crying. She was alive. Her eyelids fluttered as he lifted her over his shoulder and prayed she didn't have internal injuries. Whatever she had he couldn't wait for a stretcher or an ambulance.

He carried her up the steep slope, gasping for breath, crossed the road and placed her carefully in the back seat. She moaned and he tucked his suit jacket around her. If she was all right, he'd never let her drive that truck again. He'd never let her out of his sight again. He was responsible for this. He should never have lent them the money for the truck.

What was he thinking? Catherine was the last person in the world he could keep from doing what she wanted to do. If she wanted to drive a truck over a mountain road in the rain, she would. But why today? Why was she alone? Where was the produce? And where were the women?

The questions remained unspoken and unanswered. He made deals with himself all the way to the hospital—the things he'd tell her if she was all right, the things he'd do for her. He made deals with God, too, as he watched her being lifted into the emergency room on a gurney.

When the doctor came out, he looked serious but not grim. Josh wanted to grab him by the lapels of his lab coat and shake the news out of him. Instead he stood there and waited while the doctor found the paper he was searching for on his clipboard.

Finally he looked up. "You are the husband?"

"No," Josh said. "Not yet," he added.

The doctor nodded. "She has a concussion and three broken ribs," he said in lightly accented English.

Josh nodded automatically. "Go on," he said. "What else?"

The doctor smiled faintly. "That's all. That's enough. She must have complete rest until those ribs heal. You'll see to that?"

"I'll see to it," Josh answered emphatically.

"As for the concussion, she's drifting in and out of consciousness. She needs to be awakened every hour to see if her pupils are equal and if they react to light. We can keep her here for the night, or you can do it at home."

"I'll do it at home," he said.

"No activities that require concentration or vigorous movement," the doctor cautioned.

They brought her out in a wheelchair with a white bandage over her eye, then gave Josh a bag with her clothes and jewelry in it. She was wearing a hospital gown and his jacket over her shoulders. Her eyelids were heavy. Her lips formed his name when she saw him, but no sound came out. He clenched his hands into fists and felt tears gather in the back of his eyes.

She was so beautiful and so helpless. He'd never seen her like that before. She was the sturdy farm girl, unfazed by wind or rain. The one who led the way on the trail in her baggy pants and hiking boots. The one who had barged her way into his office and gotten a loan in spite of the rules. And now she was sitting in a wheelchair with three broken ribs and a concussion.

In front of the hospital he lifted her very gently out of the wheelchair and into his car. She drew a sharp breath, and he murmured in her ear, "Sorry, I'm sorry. Does it hurt?"

She squeezed her eyes shut tightly. "A little."

The few miles to his apartment seemed to take an eternity. He carried her into the lobby, onto the elevator and up to the penthouse. Without her heavy skirts and shawl she was as fragile as a butterfly.

Her head fell back against his arm. She was asleep again. Her eyelashes were dark smudges against her pale skin. Kneeling on the bed, he pulled back the blanket and eased her between the sheets. He leaned over and kissed her on the cheek above the cut. Even the antiseptic couldn't overpower the fresh smell of her rain-washed hair.

He put his hand on her forehead. A rush of tenderness filled him. He had to wake her every hour. Had it been an hour? No, it had only been a few minutes. He set the timer on his watch to beep every hour, then he watched her sleep.

When he woke her, she didn't want to open her eyes, but he cradled her head in his hands until she did. There were so many questions he wanted to ask, so much he had to tell her, but she went back to sleep as soon as he checked her eyes.

He made himself instant coffee and drank it as he sat in the chair at the bedroom window and watched her sleep. He dozed, his legs stretched out in front of him until his watch woke him over and over throughout the night. Each time her pupils were equal and responded to the light.

In the morning the sun rose over Teregape and streamed in his window. She opened her eyes before he told her to and stared at him in disbelief for a full minute. He got out of his chair and raked his fingers through his hair.

"Josh," she croaked. "What happened?" She touched the bandage around her head gingerly with the tips of her fingers. Her hair, a mass of dark curls, was spread out against the pillow. She'd never looked so beautiful.

He sat on the edge of the bed and traced a gentle finger around the bump on her head. "You had an accident. You broke a few ribs and hurt your head."

She groaned and looked around the room at the pale walls and the dark furniture. "Where am I?"

"My apartment. I couldn't take you home. Your ribs wouldn't stand the trip."

Her eyes strayed to the window, and a small smile tugged at the corner of her mouth. "I should have known. The bedroom with the spectacular view."

He grinned. "That's right." A giant weight was lifted from his shoulders. She remembered. She was going to be all right.

She ran her hand over the smooth percale sheets and the thick plaid comforter. "This is your bed, isn't it?" She spoke slowly, her brain still befuddled. "Where did you sleep?"

He pointed to the chair. "Right here."

She frowned. "How did I get here? What happened to the truck?"

The image of the truck smashed into the tree flashed in front of Josh's mind. "Don't worry about the truck. I brought you here in my car. When you didn't show up, I got worried about you."

She closed her eyes, and it all came back to her—the letter, the road, the rain . . . Sorrow, mingled with pain engulfed her body. How could he tell her not to worry after they sent her that letter. "I have to worry about it," she said. "So tell me what happened."

"You smashed the truck into a tree on your way down a hill. It wasn't the best day to be out driving around on steep, slick roads," he reprimanded her gently. He could afford to be gentle today. Yesterday he had been a maniac, afraid she was dead or seriously injured. Today she was safe in his bed with only three broken ribs and destined to remain there for some time whether she liked it or not. And from the look on her face she didn't like it.

Catherine saw the unperturbed expression on Josh's face, and she summoned her strength to pull herself up and glare at him. "What did you expect me to do after I got the letter? Let you come and get it? Let the whole village watch while the bank took it away?"

"What are you talking about?" he asked.

"Where are my clothes? The letter's in my pocket. Don't tell me it's not from your bank."

He found the bag the hospital had given him and opened it. In her jacket pocket was the letter. She watched his face while he read it.

"It's a form letter," he explained.

"I know it's a form letter and I know what it means. I promised you I'd bring the truck back if we had to miss a payment."

"You should have known this was a mistake. This is a final notice." He pointed to the words on the top of the letter. "Somebody pushed the wrong key on the computer. You were supposed to get the first letter because you missed one payment. The letter that asks you nicely if there's a problem to let us know so we can reschedule your payments. Why didn't you let me know?"

Tears welled up in her eyes. "I couldn't. The mailman got his truck stuck in the mud until yesterday." She blinked back her tears impatiently and lay there for a long time, gripping the edge of the comforter in her fingers and staring out the window, avoiding his gaze and feeling stupid.

"Is that why you were on the road yesterday, without the women or the produce, because you thought we were going to repossess the truck?" he asked incredulously.

She nodded and a tear slid down her cheek. "And now I've smashed it."

"Don't worry. You have insurance on it. I'll send somebody to tow it back to town."

"I should have known better." She twisted her fingers together, wishing she didn't have to meet his gaze. She stared out the window without noticing the morning sun shining on the mountain. "It was still raining in the valley when I left. The vegetables were rotting in the fields. There was nothing we could do. And then the letter came.... I took off without thinking."

He sat on the edge of the bed and wiped a tear off her cheek with his thumb. "You're alive and in one piece. Well, almost one piece. That's all that counts."

"What about the payments. We missed a payment. If it doesn't quit raining, we'll miss another one and then ..."

"And then we'll sit down and talk about it. Change the schedule, alter the interest rate. We don't want to take the truck back. We want to see you succeed."

She met his gaze at last, pressed her lips together and nodded gratefully. The look in his eyes told her more than his words how worried he'd been and how relieved he was that she was all right.

"I probably ought to be getting home now." She pulled herself up on her elbows. "Everyone will be worried about me."

He shook his head. "I'll send word back to the village with some of the women in the marketplace. They can come by to see you in a few days."

"A few days?" She looked around the room, really seeing it for the first time, the huge window with the spectacular view.

"You're not going anywhere until those ribs heal. And after that I thought I might talk you into staying around."

"Here in the city?"

"It was just an idea."

"How would you feel if I asked you to stay around with me on the farm?"

"Is that a proposal?" he asked with a gleam in his eye.

She looked up. His mouth quirked up at the corners, but his eyes turned serious. "No," she said. "Was yours?"

He nodded. "Yes."

She opened her mouth to speak, but she couldn't say a word. She put her hand on his arm. "You don't mean that. You were scared when you thought I was dead. But I'm alive, and pretty soon I'll be well and we'll go our separate ways. You rescued me and I'm grateful, but—"

"But not that grateful."

"Yes . . . no. People can't get married because they're grateful. They have to be in love." The more she said, the deeper the hole she dug for herself. Now he'd ask her if she loved him and she'd have to say yes if she were honest. It wouldn't do any good to lie. She'd been lying to herself too long. She lied to Jacinda, but Jacinda saw through her. All the women did. Josh must see it, too, her love for him shining in her eyes and hear it in her voice.

She closed her eyes and lay back on the pillow, exhausted by trying to keep her secret. Even with her eyes closed she felt his gaze on her, asking the unspoken question. She pressed her lips together to keep from blurting the answer. And then she drifted off into blissful unconsciousness.

She woke up hungry and thirsty. He brought soup and tea and watched her eat. "Where did you get this?" she asked, squinting up at him. "And where are you going?"

He straightened his tie. "I'm going to the bank for an hour. Just to check in and pick up my mail. Here's the phone. If you need me, here's the number."

She slept all afternoon, and when she woke up it was evening. From the bed she could see the lights of the city below. Josh was standing at the window, his body outlined against the glass, so tall, so strong and so wrong for her. How could fate be so cruel as to send her a man she couldn't have? Even if she canceled her five-year plan, what good would that do? How could he possibly imagine that she could live in the middle of a city, this city or any city?

Sensing she was awake, he crossed the room quietly. As he approached, she saw he was wearing a soft denim shirt and faded jeans. She wanted to feel his shirt against her face, and touch the jeans with her fingertips, feeling the hard muscles of his thighs. She hungered for his touch.

"Hungry?" he asked, as if he'd read her mind.

She smiled and held out her hand to him. He knelt there on the floor, and even in the dim light she could see the warmth in his eyes, the love and the care.

"Dinnertime," he said, and went to the kitchen. When he came back, he had baked beans and brown bread on a plate.

"These are your emergency rations," she protested, remembering from her earlier visit.

"This is an emergency," he said. "And I don't need to save them anymore. I'm going home at the end of next month. I got my promotion."

She swallowed a mouthful of beans despite the lump in her throat. "That's wonderful," she said. She was proud of her quick response, but not as proud of the way her hands shook or the sudden pounding in her head. Just when she was getting better, she felt worse. Much worse. She set her dish down and pressed her hand against her heart. Bones break, but not hearts. It was just a saying, but it was a lie.

"What is it?" he asked, easing himself onto the bed. He pressed his hand against her chest. "Do your ribs hurt?"

She nodded. "I think so." She took her hand away, but his stayed, his fingers below her breasts, sending vibrations through her body.

"I want you to come with me," he said.

"Where, to Boston?" she asked, dumbfounded.

"It doesn't have to be right in Boston. People do live outside of town and commute."

"Have you ever lived in a suburb?" she asked.

"No, but I thought it might be a good compromise," he said, outlining the opening of her hospital gown with his finger.

Trying to think rationally, she pulled the gown to her chin and tied the strings together. "How could I use everything I know, everything I've learned—grafting mutations, crop rotations—in a suburb? Besides I'm not ready to go back to the States. I can't stand to see how my parents live or what's been done to our land. Not yet."

"I'll wait."

She sighed. He had that determined look in his eyes, his chin set at a stubborn angle. She remembered how he got what he wanted. By patiently waiting. He said no more about going home or getting married or living in the suburbs. She finished her beans and bread, and he carried her out to the balcony, put her in a lounge chair and spread a blanket over her.

They listened to Andean folk music on his stereo, the reedy flutes and the stringed gourds reminding her of the outdoor restaurant. She'd never be able to hear this music without thinking of him.

What would life on the farm be like if she couldn't share with him the progress of her potatoes? How would she get along without him coming by the stall when she least expected him, sending her pulse racing and the color flooding into her cheeks?

Tears filled her eyes and blurred the lights of the city below. Fortunately he was standing at the railing of the balcony, looking out, and couldn't see that she was crying. If he did, he might think she was sad about his leaving, when she was really just sad about being stuck here in town with a bump on her head. That was all it was. Really.

When he carried her back to bed, she fell asleep and dreamed of living in the suburbs with a husband who came home at night with a newspaper under his arm and talked about banking. It wasn't a dream. It was a nightmare. Josh went to work in the morning after fixing her a piece of toast and putting the telephone next to her bed.

She tugged at the drawstrings of her gown. "I want to get out of this."

"Your clothes are in the plastic bag. But I don't think you want to wear them. Besides, you should stay right where you are."

She looked at the sliding doors of his closet. "Do you have an old shirt I can wear?"

"Help yourself," he said, and kissed her softly on the lips.

She put her arms around his neck. A pain hit her in the chest, but she ignored it. He deepened the kiss and she drank in the taste of him, memorizing the lines and angles of his face for the future. Then she sank back on the pillow, her mouth curving up in a smile.

"I'll be back for lunch," he promised.

"You come home for lunch?" she asked, surprised.

"Now I do."

After he left, she took a shower and washed her hair, very slowly and very carefully. Afterward she put on a shirt from his closet that hung down almost to her knees. It wasn't an old shirt. He didn't have any old shirts, it seemed, but she borrowed it, anyway. Exhausted from her activities, she went back to bed and fell asleep again.

She woke up when she heard the door open, then footsteps and hushed whispers. She sat up in bed. The door to the bedroom opened, and Jacinda's face appeared, followed by Doña Blanca, Margarita and the others. Josh stood behind them, looking pleased.

"How did you get here?" she asked, flinging back the blankets and swinging her legs to the floor.

They crowded forward, throwing themselves at her to exclaim over the bump on her head and the bruise on her cheek. Josh was looking at her as if he were afraid she'd break. She gave him a reassuring smile. They explained that they'd come to town with Tomás in his truck. They had come as soon as they could. They'd been frantic until they'd gotten Señor Bentley's message. Now they were relieved to see her for themselves. The rain had stopped and they had brought her some food. She must be starving. She looked so thin. They held up sacks of cheese, eggs, peppers, lettuce, potatoes and bread.

Before they left they went out onto Josh's balcony and leaned over the railing, calling to the people below. Then they looked into his giant refrigerator and turned the stove on and off to see how it worked. And as suddenly as they had come, they hurried to the door, anxious to get back to the market. Josh offered to drive them.

He stood in the doorway as they filed out. "Sorry about the lunch," he said with a rueful smile. "They appeared at the bank just as I was leaving. I didn't have time to get anything for you."

"Don't worry," she assured him. "There's enough here to feed an army."

His gaze drifted down the shirt she was wearing to her bare legs, and he nodded. "I'll be home as early as I can."

Her heart thumped against her chest. Home. It had such a nice ring to it.

It took her an hour and a half, resting often, to make a cheese soufflé and a salad for dinner. When Josh came in the door, he was carrying a newspaper under his arm just as in her dream. She gulped. Maybe dreams did come true. No, she reminded herself firmly, it wasn't a dream. It was a nightmare. He paused in the doorway to look at her, and she raised the spoon to give the salad a final toss. He came up behind her and enclosed her waist with his arms.

"Didn't I tell you you're not supposed to do anything that requires concentration or vigorous movement?" he warned. He kissed the top of her head and she closed her eyes.

"Cooking doesn't require any concentration. And I've been moving very slowly. It's taken me ages to make this simple dinner."

His hands moved up to cup her breasts under the cotton fabric of the shirt she was wearing. "I could get used to this," he said, nuzzling her neck with his lips.

"It's just a soufflé," she said breathlessly.

"That's not what I meant."

She pulled away and opened the oven to check on the soufflé. She could get used to it, too, having Josh come home every night to her. But she didn't dare. She had to get back to the farm as soon as possible, to make that break as easy as possible before she was hopelessly entangled, hopelessly in love. She was in love, she admitted to herself, but not hopelessly, not yet.

They ate on the balcony. He told her about the weavers' new alpaca sheep and about the new group of hatmakers who had just applied for a loan. They laughed. They talked. They drank coffee and lapsed into a comfortable silence. Too comfortable. Catherine stood and looked into the living room.

"Where have you been sleeping?"

"On the floor in my sleeping bag."

"I'll take the floor. I've been in your bed for days now. It's your turn."

He took his coffee and stood by the door to the balcony. "No, it isn't."

"I'm much better. I won't put you out much longer."

His eyes made a tour of the long shirt that grazed her knees. "You look better, but you're not well yet." He set his cup down and crossed the room to tilt her chin with his thumb. "What's your hurry? The women seem to be doing fine without you. The truck's being repaired. Until then they'll ride in with Tomás."

"I feel guilty. Farmers aren't allowed to get sick or take vacations. I'm restless." The first part was true. There were always cows to be milked and horses to feed. The last part wasn't. She wasn't restless. She was happy to lie in bed and look at the view from Josh's window all day, then make dinner for him at night. But she didn't want him to know how happy she was. He might get the wrong idea. And she knew that when she got well she would be restless and she'd leave.

The next night Josh brought a flat of strawberry plants the women had sent her and a clay pot. "They said they noticed my balcony had a southeast exposure, perfect for strawberries."

Catherine pressed her finger into the damp soil. "They're right," she said. The next day she planted them in the pot, a feeling of contentment stealing over her as she felt the sun on her back and the soil between her fingers.

A week went by. The women sent tomato plants next and squash seedlings until the balcony was almost full and Catherine told Josh to tell them to stop. So they sent food instead, and Catherine cooked more dinners. After dinner they talked and laughed and fell silent and thought.

"Will you water these plants when I leave?" she asked one evening.

"If you'll take them when I leave," he said.

She nodded. She didn't want to know when that was. He hadn't asked her again to go back with him. He didn't talk about going back to Boston, so she didn't, either. But she figured he didn't have many weeks left here.

He finally had to admit that she was well enough to leave. The doctor had made a final examination. The bump had receded on her forehead. The pain still came when she made a sudden movement, but the color was back in her cheeks. Wearing the cleaned and repaired pant suit she'd started out in on that rainy day, she stood and looked around the apartment, her gaze lingering on the balcony where they'd spent so much time.

Josh stood at the door, holding his breath. The pain in his chest made him wonder if he hadn't broken a few ribs, too. The past weeks had been a taste of what could be, and he wanted more, a whole lifetime more. But if she didn't feel it, didn't want it, it was better that he know now. If there was going to be a painful separation, he wanted to get it over with now.

Finally she turned and gave him a bright smile. He exhaled slowly. That was it. Nothing. This magic time had meant nothing to her. Just a brief interlude, an inconvenience. He smiled back, feeling the skin tighten at the corners of his mouth.

He drove her back to Palomar. It was a warm, sunny day, and they drove past the place where she'd gone over the bank. Only a few rocks were left on the road to remind them how slick it had been, to bring back the fear and terror he'd felt looking down through the trees.

They exchanged looks, but he didn't stop. And he didn't linger at the farm. He said he'd let her know when he got the report from the geologist on the mine, and she said she'd see him at the bank. He kissed her on the cheek and she turned and hurried into her house.

She went through the rooms, opening windows and airing them out. It was good to be back, good to be able to walk out the front door and into the fields. But at night she set two plates on the table by mistake and suddenly her eyes filled with tears. She put her head down on the kitchen table and sobbed uncontrollably for no reason.

She told herself it was a delayed reaction from the accident. She told herself she'd been holding the tears back all this time. When Josh was around, she had to be brave, but now that she was alone, there was no need. By the second day she admitted it to herself. She was alone and she was lonely.

She didn't do anything about it, though. What could she do? Tell him she missed him? Tell him she loved him? Loved him, but not enough to go back with him. Not enough to spend the rest of her life pulling weeds from a postage-stamp yard.

When they went to town, she looked for him at the bank, but when she saw him he smiled briefly and hurried away. He must be busy tying things up before he left. He looked worried and harassed. He had circles under his eyes. But then she didn't look very good, either. She hoped he didn't notice. Probably not. He never got close enough.

Jacinda got close to him. She told Catherine the truck was fixed. He'd have someone bring it to the market next week. Jacinda was the one who told her when he was leaving.

Out in the berry patch Jacinda looked puzzled. "What is wrong with Señor Bentley that he has not yet asked for your hand in marriage?" she demanded. Catherine didn't know what to say without unleashing a full-scale argument. "This is the correct way to do it," she continued, "then take you back with him."

Catherine reached across Jacinda to pick a handful of berries. "Perhaps he thinks I wouldn't go."

Jacinda pursed her lips. "What nonsense. Anyone can see you love him."

"Sometimes love isn't enough. As you know, Mr. Bentley works in the city and lives there, too. You saw his apartment. Can you imagine me in such a place?"

"If you loved him," Jacinda replied.

"I'm afraid I don't love him enough for that," Catherine said slowly.

"There is only one way to find out," Jacinda said.

Catherine waited, but Jacinda didn't say what that was.

The day before he was to leave Catherine hadn't gotten the plants from Josh's balcony, nor had she heard from him about the results from the mine. So instead of riding home with the women, she gathered her courage and went to Josh's apartment. He wasn't there, but the doorman remembered her and let her into the penthouse. The living room was full of boxes, the same boxes she'd helped him open only a short time ago.

She thought of the picture of his father and how he'd come to terms with his inheritance. It no longer seemed important to him if the mine paid off or not except for the others. For himself he'd found something more valuable—his father's memory.

She sat in the dark on the floor of the balcony, her body trembling, waiting for him. She was trying to decide what to say. She held her hands up to her eyes to block out the peripheral light so she could locate Scorpio, the constellation that had gotten her into this situation in the first place.

She pictured herself on the farm where she'd grown up, but the outlines of the house and the fields were just as fuzzy as the outline of Scorpio. It had been almost two years since she'd left the land of her birth. Long enough to grieve over the lost land and her lost heritage. Josh had learned to put his loss behind him and move on. Wasn't it time she did the same?

The front door opened. Josh stumbled on a box in the dark and swore. She jumped to her feet. The door swung closed behind him. She waited while his eyes grew accustomed to the darkness, wiping her damp palms against her skirt.

"I didn't know anyone was here," he said after a pause.

"The doorman let me in. I didn't want you to leave without..." All of a sudden her nerve deserted her and she faltered.

He crossed the room and joined her on the balcony. "Without saying goodbye. Of course. I meant to come by the market, but they had a surprise party after work. Then it was too late. I thought you'd have left."

His voice was cool and reserved. How could he talk to her that way if he really loved her?

She looked around at the bare walls, at the hallway to the bedroom, toward the kitchen. "I've missed you," she said, the pain rising in her chest. "I've missed this place."

He stared at her. "I thought you hated this place."

"I thought I did, too. But I discovered I'd rather live in the city with you than anywhere else without you."

"Even Boston?" he asked incredulously, afraid to believe his ears.

She felt her lips curve into a smile. She hadn't smiled much since she'd left this place weeks ago. "Even Boston."

He put his arms around her and held her tightly. "Is that a proposal?"

She slid her arms around his neck. "I know I'm supposed to wait until you ask my parents for my hand, but I'm an American, and American women sometimes take matters into their own hands."

"Thank God," he muttered against her ear.

"I'm not free for three months, though. Until then I belong to the Peace Corps."

He pulled back to see happiness spilling from her dark eyes. If she didn't have three ribs still mending, he would have crushed her to him and swung her around the living room.

"I'll need three months to find a place for us to live, someplace with a field or an orchard that's within commuting distance to the city," he said.

She pressed her hands together, unable to resist the tidal wave of joy that threatened to engulf her. All this and green grass, too.

"Josh," she said. "It doesn't matter. I meant what I said. I'll live anywhere with you. I came here to teach people how to farm. But I learned much more—how to let go of what's gone, and how to love. You can't take all the credit," she said, taking his face in her hands. "Just most of it." She brought his mouth down to hers and gave him the most profound kiss he'd ever had.

Moments later he broke away and looked down at her. "If you were completely well . . ." he said shakily.

"I've never felt better in my life," she assured him.

He lifted her into his arms. "Are you trying to get me to take you back to that bed in there?" His eyes were smoky blue.

"Mmm," she answered, lowering her mouth to his for another kiss.

He stopped at the doorway to the bedroom. "Catherine," he said, "you still can't do anything that requires vigorous movement or concentration."

"Those are the only kinds of things I want to do."

"Me, too, but we'll wait until your ribs are back together again. I'll give you three months to heal and plan the wedding."

She gazed off dreamily. "It'll be like Magdalena's in the village church." He set her on the bed, and she looked up at him, her eyes wide and luminous. "Sleep with me," she said. "I thought about you sleeping in this bed with me every night I spent here." She saw the worry lines form in his forehead. "No vigorous movements," she promised. "Just hold me. All night long."

She wore his one clean shirt that wasn't packed and her cotton bikini panties. He wore the flannel shirt he was planning to leave behind and pin-striped boxer shorts. Josh pulled the comforter up over them, carefully tucking it over her shoulders. He held her gently, as if she might break, remembering the time when she almost did.

She shifted to feel the weight of his body against hers. His hard planes and muscles pressed against her soft hollows. She sighed with happiness.

His hand cupped her breast and he felt her heart race. He couldn't sleep. He wouldn't sleep until he got on the plane tomorrow. "Oh, no. I almost forgot."

She turned to face him. "What?"

"The report from the geologist."

"It must not be good news or you wouldn't have forgotten."

"Good news and bad news. The bad news is that there was no silver in any of the samples. The good news is that the rock you picked up is zinc, ruby zinc, to be exact. You have good taste in rocks." He caressed her bottom lip with his thumb.

"Why, is it valuable?" She absorbed his touch and the clean male scent of his skin.

"It is if there's enough of it. So they're going to send a team to do a survey."

"That would be the icing on the cake," she said, her cheek against his. "So it does work."

He inhaled the fragrance of her hair, still unable to believe that she was here in his bed, in his arms. "What?" he asked lazily.

"Sleeping on a piece of wedding cake. I dreamed about you that night."

He kissed her eyelids. "Will you dream about me tonight?"

"Every night," she promised. "Until you get back."

Epilogue

A hush fell over the small village church when the bride appeared on the arm of her father. Her dress was white satin and had been worn by her mother and her grandmother before her. The women whispered that her mother had brought it on the plane all the way from California.

The groom's blue eyes never left the face of his bride. They'd been separated these past few months, and he drank in the sight of her like a thirsty man who'd been too long in the desert. The service was in Spanish, but the vows were in English. The kiss was all-American, all-promising and all-consuming.

The guests who threw tiny grains of wheat at the couple in front of the church were dressed in their Sunday best. The men, home from the mines for good, wore their dark suits for the second time in recent months.

The reception was held at Jacinda's, where a tent had been set up to protect the guests from the sun and shade the bountiful buffet the women had been preparing all week.

Catherine introduced Old Pedro to her father. "He's the richest man in town," she explained, "with his shares of the zinc mine."

Pedro looked down at his scuffed shoes. "Money does not buy happiness," he told them. "I was happy before the mine was reopened. I am still happy. Fixing drainpipes, making gutters. But for them…" He waved a gnarled hand at the men clustered around the barbecue in their shiny suits. "The money from the shares belonging to their fathers and grandfathers has changed their lives. They have come back to work in the village where they belong. To help with the plowing, or building or keeping their wives happy." His smile revealed a gap between his front teeth.

Catherine realized she'd never noticed it because she'd never seen him smile before. He wasn't the only one smiling. On the other side of the tent Jacinda took Josh aside to extend her congratulations. Josh didn't think anyone could be happier than he was, but Jacinda was basking in the glow of another successful wedding. And she wasn't too shy to take all the credit for it.

"Señor Bentley," she said, twisting her gold necklace around her fingers. "I remember the first day I saw you with the mangoes in your hand. It was then I knew you were destined for our Catalina. Since that time I have worked long and hard for this day." She sighed dramatically and wiped her forehead with her handkerchief.

Josh was glad he remembered enough Spanish to thank her profusely for her efforts. When the brass band began to play, she waltzed away to join the dancers. Beyond the twirling figures of the guests, Josh saw Catherine framed by her parents on either side of her. When he reached her, her mother drew a glass jar from a bag and presented it to Catherine.

"It's just dirt from the farm," she explained. "I saved it for you. I thought you might want it—" her voice caught "—for sentimental reasons."

Catherine held the jar up and gazed at the dirt inside reverently. "Look," she said to Josh, "I can use it to start my garden at our new house." Her eyes misted over as she looked from her father to her mother.

"We knew you thought it was wrong to sell," her mother said.

Catherine shook her head, unable to speak.

"But we did what we thought was best," her father finished.

Catherine hugged her mother tightly. "I know that. And what's even better than the dirt are the memories you gave me of a happy childhood. Nobody can ever take them away from me." She looked over her mother's shoulder at her new husband. "Ask Josh. He's heard about the barn kittens and the sweaters you knit me until he can't take any more."

"Not true," he assured her. "I can take a lot more. Just try me. How about a dance, Señora Bentley?"

She looked around. "Who, me?"

He took her into his arms. The brass band had retired and the guitarist played a Spanish love song. They moved across the patio in time to the music, and he gazed into her eyes as if they were alone under the tent, with the breeze blowing the scent of fresh hay from the fields.

"Have I told you how glad I am I came to this country?" he said with his lips against her ear.

"You found the treasure you've been looking for all your life," she murmured.

"You're so right," he said, his hand against the white satin, pressing her close.

She blushed. "I meant the mine." She held up her hand to look at the ring he had made from the rock she had discovered in the mine.

"That, too. The zinc, my father, myself and you. And not necessarily in that order."

She smiled against his cheek. "I showed my parents the picture of our new house. They think on five acres I can grow enough hay for a couple of cows and a horse or two."

He moved his head to look in her eyes. "Save room for the pair of llamas I'm giving you."

Her eyes filled with tears again. "Oh, Josh, really?"

"Really. They're waiting for you at the breeder's." He guided her expertly toward the shade of the grape arbor. "By the way, who's going to take care of all these animals?"

She thought a moment. "The children?"

He raised his eyebrows. "How many?"

"Oh, four or five. As many as possible."

He kissed her and tasted the sweetness of the icing on the wedding cake. "We'd better get started," he said. "As soon as possible."

* * * * *

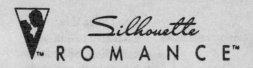

COMING NEXT MONTH

#886 A CHANGED MAN—Karen Leabo *Written in the Stars*
Conservative Virgo man Stephen Whitfield was too uptight for
impulsive Sagittarius Jill Ballantine. But Jill sensed a lovable man
beneath that stuffy accountant exterior. All Stephen needed was a
little loosening up!

#887 WILD STREAK—Pat Tracy
Erin Clay had always been off-limits to Linc Severance—first as his
best friend's wife and then as his best friend's widow. Now Linc was
back in town . . . and ready to test the forbidden waters.

#888 YOU MADE ME LOVE YOU—Jayne Addison
Nothing Caroline Phelps ever did seemed to turn out right—*except*
meeting sexy Jack Corey. But when life's little disasters began to
occur, could Caroline trust Jack to always be there?

#889 JUST ONE OF THE GUYS—Jude Randal
Dana Morgan was a do-it-yourself woman—more at home in a
hardware store than in a beauty parlor. But Spencer Willis was out to
prove there *was* one thing Dana couldn't do alone . . . fall in love!

#890 MOLLY MEETS HER MATCH—Val Whisenand
To Molly Evans, Brian Forrester was a gorgeous male specimen. So
what if he was in a wheelchair? But she *couldn't* ignore his stubborn
pride—or his passion . . . even if she wanted to.

#891 THE IDEAL WIFE—Joleen Daniels
Sloan Burdett wanted Lacey Sue Talbert like no woman on earth, but
if he was going to have her, he'd have to move fast. Lacey Sue was
about to walk down the aisle with his brother. . . .

AVAILABLE THIS MONTH:

#880 BABY SWAP
Suzanne Carey

#881 THE WIFE HE WANTED
Elizabeth August

**#882 HOME IS WHERE THE
HEART IS**
Carol Grace

**#883 LAST CHANCE FOR
MARRIAGE**
Sandra Paul

#884 FIRE AND SPICE
Carla Cassidy

**#885 A HOLIDAY TO
REMEMBER**
Brittany Young

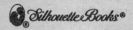

NORA ROBERTS

Love has a language all its own, and for centuries, flowers have symbolized love's finest expression. Discover the language of flowers—and love—in this romantic collection of 48 favorite books by bestselling author Nora Roberts.

Two titles are available each month at your favorite retail outlet.

In August, look for:

Tempting Fate, **Volume #13**
From this Day, **Volume #14**

In September, look for:

All the Possibilities, **Volume #15**
The Heart's Victory, **Volume #16**

THE **LANGUAGE** of **LOVE**

Collect all 48 titles
and become fluent in

Silhouette®

Back by popular demand...

TELL ME NO LIES

In a world
full of deceit
and manipulation,
truth is a double-
edged sword.

Lindsay Danner is the
only one who can lead the
search for the invaluable
Chinese bronzes. Jacob
Catlin is the only one who
can protect her. They
hadn't planned on
falling in love....

Available in August at
your favorite retail outlet.

ELIZABETH LOWELL

Silhouette
R O M A N C E ™